NEVER DATE A DOCTOR

A LIFE LESSONS NOVEL

MELANIE A. SMITH

WICKED DREAMS PUBLISHING

Published by
WICKED DREAMS PUBLISHING
info@wickeddreamspublishing.com
Boise, ID USA

Edited by Jennifer Gardner

Cover design by Wicked Dreams Publishing

Formatting by Wicked Dreams Publishing

eBook (K) ISBN: 978-1-7323900-8-9
eBook ISBN: 978-1-7330748-8-9

Paperback ISBN: 978-1-7323900-9-6
Hardback ISBN: 978-1-952121-06-7

CONTENTS

1

"So what's it going to take, Sasha?" Becca asks pointedly before taking another sip of coffee.

I shoot her a pointed grimace. "I'm not asking for fucking Henry Cavill," I grouse. "Is it really too much to want a good, steady guy who treats me well but also makes my toes curl and my lady bits swoon when I see him?"

She arches an eyebrow and thinks about that as she continues to drink her coffee. Way too slowly for the small break we're allotted. I tap my fingers impatiently next to my empty coffee cup. Finally, she finishes and sets hers on the peeling laminate tabletop.

"Yes," she says flatly, rising to rinse her cup. "Because the type of guy who curls *your* toes is going to know he's hot shit. And that doesn't exactly translate to boyfriend material."

"Oh? And what exactly is my *type*?" I rise from my chair, setting my coffee mug back in its usual spot without rinsing it. Lord knows I'm going to be back in here for another cup soon anyway.

"'Henry Cavill' says it all, my dear," she replies airily as she heads back into the main office. "Tall, dark, handsome, blue eyes, rockin' bod. *Your type.* You set your standards too damn high and you're stuck in a no-dating rut."

I frown deeply as I approach the intake station and grab the chart slotted into my cubby. I'm not exactly in a position to argue, as she's not wrong. But having it pointed out so bluntly is beyond annoying. Just because I hold out for my "type" doesn't mean I'm hopelessly stuck.

"It's called having standards," I respond drily. "I can define that if it's unclear."

"So are you ever going to tell me *why*

that's a type you can't seem to break away from?" she teases, totally ignoring my not-so-subtle dig as she settles in at the nurses' station. Her eyes suddenly widen. "Oh god, that's not what your dad looks like, is it?"

My eyes flick up from the chart in my hands.

"Becca, that's disgusting." I gesture to my dark blond hair. "Besides, where do you think I got this?"

She shrugs and grins mischievously. "Good. Because daddy issues are a whole other ballgame. So who was it? First boyfriend? First lay? Both?" Her eyebrows waggle suggestively.

This time I slam the folder closed. "Christ, Becks, keep your voice down." My eyes dart around, hoping nobody else heard her.

"Oh, this must be good, you little prude, you," she says, greedily rubbing her hands together.

"I'm not a *prude*," I protest. "I just don't talk about my sex life at work. Or jump into bed with every guy I date." I shoot her a meaningful, if not teasing, stare.

"Maybe you should give it a try sometime.

It's every bit as fun as it sounds," she retorts with a wink. "Fine, have it your way. Go to your ten a.m., but we're having drinks after work, and I *am* getting this story."

"Have it your way," I reply mockingly, "just so long as you're buying."

"I think I will have it my way, thank you very much," she replies airily. But then her eyes go wide as she looks over my shoulder.

I turn to see the chief of our unit headed at us, a stern frown on his grey-bearded face. He's always in a shit mood, and I know I need to get in to see my patient before I become his next target.

"Dr. MacDougall is all you, Becks," I whisper with a sly grin before shooting into exam room seven. I just catch her annoyed glare as I close the door behind me.

"I SWEAR. I LOVE MY JOB, BUT IF ONE MORE old man tries to feel me up while I'm doing an echo, I'm going to respond with violence." I take a huge gulp of the martini in front of me, knowing even that won't wash away the memory of his wrinkled paw squeezing my ass.

Becca shoots me a sympathetic look from across the small table we're perched at. It barely fits our drinks, and the place is packed, but I guess I should've realized that, as it's a Friday night. I just don't pay much attention to the days of the week anymore, unless it's a school night. The hazards of working at a cardiac unit that's open seven days a week while going to school to graduate from nurse to nurse-practitioner. My days have two classifications: non-school days that are just long and difficult, and school days which are so grueling they could be considered a form of torture. Christ, I'm such a masochist.

"Been there," Becca agrees. "But honestly, I wouldn't have even minded. It's been way too long since I've had *any* action."

I laugh incredulously. "I find that hard to believe."

She shrugs. "Oh, believe it. Even I go through dry spells. And you know what they say about desperate times …" She looks around at the crowds wistfully before her eyes wander back to mine. "If only there were anyone here worth going after. But we have other business to get to anyway. Now. About Henry Cavill."

"What about him? Did you want to go see a movie after this?" I dodge jokingly.

One of Becca's perfectly shaped eyebrows lifts. I throw up my hands in defeat.

"Fine. But you're going to make fun of me."

"*Moi*? I would never." The evil glint in her eye belies her innocent tone. "Seriously, though, out with it. I'm on a mission here to get us both laid."

"Getting laid isn't really an issue," I reply with a shrug. At five-and-a-half feet, with blond hair and curves in all the right places, attracting male attention has never been a problem. The opposite, in fact, especially working in the medical profession. Though frankly I think just being female is enough, since I know most of the other nurses and MAs at work have to deal with the same crap. You'd think it was still 1950, not 2020, the way some of these old bastards behave. And in a facility that deals exclusively with heart problems, we pretty much get mostly elderly patients.

"So out with it," Becca prompts. "Maybe we can cleanse you of your need for Superman."

I stick my tongue out at her, and she laughs.

"Fine," I reply with a sigh. "But if I tell you, you have to promise not to laugh."

Becca presses her lips together in amusement and gestures for me to continue, twirling her dark brown hair around a finger while her equally dark brown eyes survey me. We've worked together at the cardiac unit for too many years — she was already a medical assistant when I started there during nursing school — and have been friends just as long, so she knows me better than almost anybody. But this … this, I've never told *anyone*.

I down the rest of my drink. What the hell. Here goes.

"When I was fourteen, I went to my first airshow sans parents," I begin. Becca grins widely. I don't have to explain the significance of that to her; she grew up in San Diego too, attending the annual airshow just the same as I always have. Ogling the hot guys on offer, in uniform and out. Going on your own meant the chance to flirt unimpeded by parental units.

"So, your Henry was a hunky sailor, huh?" she teases.

I shrug. "I don't know," I reply honestly. "He wasn't in uniform. We didn't even speak. My friends were pulling me toward the hangar, and I looked up and there he was. He was with a group of guys heading the other direction."

I close my eyes, bringing up the mental picture that hasn't faded in detail, despite it being ten years ago.

"He was older than me, maybe late teens? But he had dark-brown hair and the most beautiful, clear blue eyes I'd ever seen. Seriously, when we locked eyes, I froze in place. I couldn't move. He was so gorgeous. So fucking perfect. But mostly ..." I open my eyes to see Becca staring, enraptured.

"What?" she prompts impatiently.

I scrunch up my nose. In for a penny ...

"I felt *it*," I admit on a sigh. "A tug in my chest. Like the world dropped away, and it was just us. Like the universe went quiet so I could hear the pounding of my heart. Feel the connection between us like it was a living thing." I lean back, lamenting my empty glass. "And then my friends pulled me away and I lost him in the crowd."

Becca sits up straight, her face dropping.

"That's it? You saw some guy during fleet week ten years ago who got your hormones going and you're spoiled for anyone who doesn't have dark hair and blue eyes? Fuck, Sash, that's nuts."

"And that's me, done for the night," I reply, rising from my seat.

She reaches out and grabs my hand, pulling me back as I retreat. "I'm sorry," she replies. "Please, stay. I'll even buy you another drink."

A small smile finds its way onto my lips, and I sink back into the chair.

"You're forgiven. But I swear I'm not crazy. I don't think I date guys who look like that because of him. I think that's just what I find attractive. But what I can't seem to find is something that moves me the way looking into his eyes did." I pause, trying to figure out how to explain it. I look back up, and Becca is staring at me curiously. "It was like … seeing a stranger, but knowing everything about him was just there, waiting for me to know. And everything in me *wanted* that, wanted to know him. Like it would be the answer to everything." I can tell by the look on her face that she totally doesn't get where I'm coming from, so I just stop, shaking my head.

"I can't say I understand," she replies slowly. "But that's cool. I mean, I get wanting to really feel something with someone. But I guess I didn't realize you were such a fucking romantic."

I laugh at Becca's talent for keeping things from getting too serious. "I'm really not. It was just a thing that happened. But it's always stuck in my head. Like that's the way it should be. That's how I should feel when I meet the right guy."

"So that's why you've only had a handful of relationships that never lasted longer than a few months the whole time I've known you?"

"I don't know. I guess I always chalked that up to focusing on school, and my career. And, I mean, I'm only twenty-four. But I guess, yeah, I've never really felt that again. I'm not stupid, though, Becks. It's not like I don't give guys a chance. Even if there's not that initial spark. I try to stick around, waiting for it. But it never comes."

"Wow," Becca mouths.

"Have you ever felt that way?" I ask, suddenly wondering if something is wrong with me.

"I've been attracted to guys. Wanted to jump their bones. Well, actually jumped their bones," she allows. "But I can't say I've ever had my *universe go quiet*."

"Fuck you, Becca. Fuck you." Becca, thankfully, is extremely difficult to offend, and she just laughs in response.

"You wish," she jokes with a wink. "You know I don't swing that way."

"Me neither. But wouldn't that just solve both of our problems," I tease back with my own wink.

2

The next morning I fill my coffee mug to the brim and stifle a yawn as I head into our mandated morning staff tag-up. Becca joins me as I pass the nurses' station, cradling her own giant cup of java.

"Someday," she sighs, "I'll have a job where I don't have to be in at six a.m. on a Saturday. I wonder what MacDougall wants, anyway."

"There's a new doc on the block," a cheery voice comes from behind us.

We both look back to see my supervisor, Julianna Magnusson, approaching, looking every inch the morning person she is, all bright-eyed with a pep in her step. Well, supervisor, mentor, and friend. None of us would make it without Jules. She's been a nurse practitioner at Rutherford Hospital for ten years and was a nurse here for six before that. She knows more than just about anyone at the hospital how things run across units. Which also makes her privy to the best gossip.

"Yeah? Any dirt?" Becca asks gleefully as Jules joins us.

Jules sweeps her burgundy hair into a ponytail with a quiet smile. "Only that he's coming from Cedars-Sinai in L.A., where he also apparently did his cardiac surgery training." Becca gives her a disappointed look and Jules laughs. "Sorry, babes, I bumped into Dr. MacDougall and that was all he had time to tell me. We're all about to find out anyway."

Becca gives an indifferent shrug, clearly having wanted to know before everyone else, and Jules and I share a look as we enter the staff meeting room. We seem to be the last in, aside from Dr. MacDougall and our new addition. Becca sniffs the air suspiciously.

"Oh god, what is it?" I ask. In a hospital,

you never know what an odd smell is going to lead to.

Becca takes another deep sniff and her eyes go wide. "Donuts!" And she's off, dragging me across the room to where, behind a cluster of MAs, there are, in fact, two huge boxes of donuts.

"Damn, Becks, you're a freaking bloodhound," I tease as she grabs the nearest donut and stuffs it in her face.

"Oh my god, they're still warm," she groans around a mouthful of pastry.

"You're a nutjob," I say with a laugh.

"Good morning, everybody," Dr. MacDougall's voice booms from behind me.

I spin in place at his clear call to order. As the room quiets, my eyes fall on our chief … and a man I've never seen before standing next to him. It takes my brain about two seconds when a loud gasp of recognition escapes me. Everyone turns to look, including him, and I blush deeply. Thankfully, Dr. MacDougall clears his throat, bringing the attention back to the front of the room. As he starts his usual greeting speech, Becca leans in.

"What was that all about?" she whispers.

I turn toward her so she can see the shock on my face, and my hand finds hers, gripping it tightly.

"It's *him*," I hiss. Becca gives me a confused look, and I roll my eyes. *"Universe Guy."*

Becca gives me a skeptical look, her eyes turning back to the front. Taking in what I did. All six-feet-two-ish inches of the dark-haired, blue-eyed, and unquestionably sexy hunk of a well-built man in blue scrubs and a white lab coat standing next to Dr. MacDougall as he rambles about our round stats for the week.

"Are you sure?" she whispers back. "Maybe you just *think* it's Universe Guy because we were just talking about him."

With a lump in my throat, I chance another look at him. Thankfully, his eyes are roaming the crowd as Dr. MacDougall gives his usual boring speech that is now shifting toward a lecture on proper chart notes. The young man I remember was clean-shaven, and though this guy has a well-trimmed beard that defines his sharp jaw, otherwise it's the exact face I remember, just a bit older. Same broad shoulders. Same trim waist. Though he's filled out in the chest and arms, and I can practically see the muscles straining against the fabric of his shirt. But I've got the same butterflies in my stomach.

"I don't know. I'm pretty sure it's him," I mumble. As if he heard me, his eyes land on me. And the sound of Dr. MacDougall droning on muffles under the pounding of my heart in my ears. My insides tighten. And, for the second time in my life, the universe goes quiet. A surge of emotion pounds through me, even stronger than the one ten years ago. I've never reacted to anyone this way, and it's equal parts terrifying and thrilling, and I can't stop staring back into his baby blues.

But when his eyes snap away suddenly, the volume comes rushing back. And I notice that my heart is pounding and I'm breathing like I just ran sprints. I take a deep breath to steady myself, hoping nobody noticed my ridiculous reaction to him.

"… and so, finally, I'd like to introduce the newest addition to our team, specializing in cardiac surgery, Dr. Thompson. Though he was heavily recruited out of his residency with Cedars-Sinai, he chose to stay there — until now. We are extremely lucky to have him, so please join me in welcoming him to our team."

A smattering of applause rings around the room, and I clap my hands together with them, but I'm completely numb with shock.

Dr. Thompson puts a hand up in greeting, and the room once again falls silent.

"Thank you, everyone," he says. And my jaw drops at the unmistakably posh British accent. "I'm Dr. Caleb Thompson. As you've probably noticed, I'm not originally from Los Angeles." A few in the crowd, mostly females, titter at his comment. "I graduated from Cambridge seven years ago now, then moved to the States for my residency. While I enjoyed my time at Cedars-Sinai, I'm already very impressed with Rutherford Hospital, and I'm pleased to be working with you all. I will be making my rounds to get to know each of you throughout the day. But first, may I ask, who are my surgical nurses?" Jules' hand goes up, as do several others. "Excellent. Good to put faces to the names on my sheet." He holds a clipboard aloft with a smile that gets another few titters from the peanut gallery. But my heart is in my shoes.

He moved here seven years ago. He can't be Universe Guy. My eyes scan his face as he continues to talk about how he plans to integrate into established routines, consultations, and the like, but all I can think about is how much he looks like The Guy. I even had the same reaction. And then some. By the time he's done and we've all been dismissed, I'm dumbly zoning out in my own bubble of confusion.

I feel a tug on my elbow as Becca tries to get my attention.

"Hey, I have to start processing patients. You okay?" I finally look up to see the look of pity on her face. She's clearly also realized he can't possibly be the same guy from my story.

"Sure, yeah," I mumble. "Sorry. I just could've sworn it was him."

Becca gives a light shrug. "Probably better that it isn't," she says gently. "After all, what's the first rule of Nurses' Club?"

That gets a smile out of me. "Never talk about Nurses' Club?" I tease.

She wrinkles her nose and jiggles her

head. "That just gets funnier every time I hear it," she replies wryly, then gives me an expectant look.

"I know, I know," I reply with a sigh. "Never date a doctor."

It's been drilled into me so many times. Not because it's against policy; it's not. But the relationship between doctors and their support staff is already difficult at best, and lives are literally on the line every day. Even in my time here, I see the wisdom of not complicating that further. Not that it matters. Even if he was Universe Guy, what chance would I have with a guy like that?

"That's right, boo," Becca says. "Chin up." She shoots a look at Dr. Thompson, who is deep in conversation with Jules. "If it helps, there are still donuts left."

A little chuckle escapes me, and it snaps me back to reality. What am I even doing thinking about this guy? He's not who I thought he was. He's now a doctor in our unit. Even if he was interested, it's *not* going to happen. And while I hadn't been planning on having one, I decide a donut sounds pretty damn good.

"It does help," I reply with a grateful smile. "Thanks, Becks. See you in a bit."

She gives me a wink and slips out the door. I grab the last glazed donut and follow suit, not even looking at Dr. Hottie on my way out. It's better that way, because I have a feeling being too close to him wouldn't go well for me.

But Jules apparently has other ideas.

"Sasha," she calls as I step over the threshold, "come meet Dr. Thompson."

I turn slowly on the spot to find Jules staring at me expectantly. Dr. Thompson is looking at me, a half-smile on his face as he studies me curiously. His eyes sweeping casually over me sends chills down my spine.

"Of course," I reply, clearing my throat and switching the donut to my left hand so I can extend my right as I step toward them. "It's a pleasure to meet you, Dr. Thompson."

His large, warm hand slips into mine, and my insides do their little clenching thing again. He may not be who I thought he was, but, as Becca teased me about on Friday, I have a type. And he's definitely it. I swallow hard and try not to let the nervous tension I feel affect my smile as I look up into his eyes. It doesn't work, and I push back against the well of want that is bubbling up inside of me.

"Sasha … Suvorin?" he guesses.

I clear my throat, willing back my body's reaction. "You're a quick study," I reply.

His answering laugh is warm and rich, and does nothing to help me forget how attractive he is. "I am a doctor. We pretty much just memorize things for a living." I'd like to respond, but for a moment all I can think is, *Damn, that accent is sexy as hell.* His hand lingers in mine for a little longer than is strictly necessary. Jules looks between us both, and I withdraw my hand self-consciously.

"I have some experience with that. I'm working toward my master's in nursing, and it's pretty much the same," I finally reply, finding myself again.

His eyebrows jump and a slow smile spreads across his lips. I can't help but stare, noting his bottom lip is fuller than the top. I watch him tuck it into his mouth, the hair under the center of his lip moving with it. It's undeniably sexy.

"Ah, yes, getting your MSN? That's love-ly," he replies. And the way he says "lovely," I know I'm going to be repeating it to myself in his accent for the rest of the morning. "So I don't detect a Russian accent, despite the surname …"

I smile tolerantly. I get that a lot. To the extent of actual strangers full on speaking to me in Russian like I should understand. "My grandparents came here many years ago, and my parents preferred we speak English at home so I didn't have any trouble at school. I'm afraid I know about as much Russian as Jules here."

Jules smiles at me right as Dr. Franklin, one of our cardiologists, pops into the room. "Cal, my first consult is here. Join me?"

Dr. Thompson — or Cal, apparently — gives him a sharp nod.

"I expect I'll be seeing you both around," he says to Jules and me.

"Of course," Jules pipes chirpily.

"Yes, nice meeting you," I reply softly, but he's already headed out the door. Thank god. I finally relax, the weird pull he has on my hormones now absent.

Jules fans herself dramatically. "Is it hot in here or was it just him?" she gushes. "Whew! And he seems so *nice*. Definitely trouble with a capital T, that one."

My gut twinges unpleasantly, and I turn to toss the donut in the garbage, having completely lost my appetite.

"He seems okay," I say with a shrug.

Jules smirks at me knowingly. "Oh please, if eye contact was a sex act, you two would've just gotten to third base."

"He's too old for me," I protest. Or at least, I assume he is.

Jules snorts as she heads out the door, so I follow along. "He's about my age," she scoffs. "And I'm only ten years older than you. That's no biggie."

"Except he's a doctor, and —"

"Yeah, yeah, yeah, never date a doctor. I practically invented that rule, Sasha. And do you know why?"

I look up at her, since she's a good four inches taller than me, not sure if this is a trap. "Why?"

"Because I've dated enough doctors to know better."

"Precisely," I respond. "So it doesn't matter how old he is. It's not like either of us is going to date him."

Jules cackles. "No, Sasha, *I've* dated enough doctors to know better. That's part of the fun of having rules: breaking them to find out why they're rules in the first place."

I shoot her a concerned look as we approach the supply closet. "I'm not sure how I feel about someone responsible for so many people's lives on a daily basis having that kind of attitude," I tease. Well, mostly tease. Jules is usually one of the most cautious people I know, so I find this reversal oddly confusing.

She waves a hand at me as we start prepping our supplies for the day.

"You know I would never endanger a patient. I'm not talking about that. I'm talking about you," she replies seriously, maintaining firm but kind eye contact as she mechanically sorts syringes. "You're so serious, so focused. If someone catches your eye, don't write them off because of a rule that's not even really a rule. You never know. That's all I'm saying."

I raise an eyebrow. "I happen to like

focusing on things that really matter," I reply archly. "Ever since I started volunteering at this hospital as a teenager, I've always known this is what I wanted to do. I like focusing on it." And not getting distracted by ridiculously hot doctors.

"I know, Sash," she says, handing me a stack of dressing gowns. "Just don't be so focused that you miss out on other opportunities that are part of the human experience." She winks at me, and I find myself a little aggravated. I may not be the most social person, but I've dated. I've gotten out. I mean, not exactly frequently these days, but she's talking like I'm eschewing men and I need to drop everything to go after this one because we made some flirty eye contact. She doesn't need to know about the other stuff, it would just encourage her.

So instead of arguing, I just shake my head and wheel the stocked cart away, intent on focusing on what I always focus on: my job.

It's not long before Becca catches up with me, as I'm cleaning instruments in the sterilization area.

"Hey, Dr. C is looking for you," she tells me.

I raise an eyebrow. Dr. Carson is my least favorite cardiologist on the unit. He's *extremely* particular about how his exam rooms are set up and shoves most of his work off on the nurses regularly. Not that that's terribly unusual, it's just extra annoying because of his attitude.

"Gee, well, I'll just jump right over then," I reply sarcastically, wrapping the scalpel in my hand in muslin before setting it in the sterilization tray. "You know. In a little while."

Becca leans back against the counter with a chuckle. "I thought you might say that." She taps a long fingernail on her arm thoughtfully. "So, Dr. Thompson might not be your Universe Guy, but he's still pretty cute, right?"

I roll my eyes. "If you and Jules think he's such hot stuff, you guys should go after him."

"Jules thinks he's hot?"

"What female in that room didn't?" I reply with a shrug. "He was hot even before he opened his mouth."

Becca sighs dreamily. "Yeah, that accent

is pretty amazing." She shudders dramatically.

I wrap the last instrument and settle it in the tray, then slide the tray into the autoclave and switch it on. We both step back to let it do its thing.

"Look. I get it. He's my type. He's hot. He's British. But he's also a doctor, a coworker, and too old for me. I appreciate that you guys want me to find a guy, but I promise that I'm *happy* being single."

Becca looks past me, agape. On instinct, I turn around. And Dr. Caleb Thompson is standing in the doorway with a look on his face that says he heard everything. I internalize a heavy sigh. Yep. That's about right. That's pretty much how things go for me when it comes to men I might potentially be interested in.

"Is there something I can help you with, Dr. Thompson?" I ask as evenly as I can, but inside I'm dying. Becca skitters out of the room, just squeezing by him. The fucking traitor.

"I'm sorry, I — I didn't mean to interrupt anything, I'll just ... I can come back later

…" He's clearly horribly embarrassed, as he's stumbling over every other word.

Despite my best efforts, I feel the heat creep up my cheeks. "No, I'm sorry. We shouldn't have been —"

"It's okay, I really should … I can come back later." He turns, but I stop him with a hand on his arm.

"Please, can we just pretend like that never happened?" I shift nervously from foot to foot as his gaze meets mine. His clear blue eyes search mine for a moment, and my stomach flip-flops.

"I'm sorry, pretend what never happened?" he replies with a small smile.

Some of the tension in my shoulders lift at his obvious out.

"You needed something?" I prompt, but still pretty much just wanting this to be over with so I can go crawl in a hole and die.

"Yes, of course," he replies, finding himself again. "I wanted to acquaint myself with the supplies, since I needed a few things anyway. I have a catheter angiography this afternoon."

"Well, I'm happy to show you where

everything is, but one of us will take care of all of that for you," I assure him.

"I'm perfectly happy to, especially at first. It'll be good for me to get to know where things are and how everything works, just in case."

Ugh. Seriously? As if his mere presence doesn't reduce me to an idiotic mess, he's also willing to do menial work that most doctors, especially surgeons, see as a waste of their time. They almost always expect the nurses to take care of everything that doesn't strictly require an M.D. I mean, I get it, there are more nurses per patient than doctors, but still. He couldn't just be smart and gorgeous, he had to be considerate too. And against my better judgment, I want to know more about him.

"In that case, I'll give you the grand tour," I reply. I can only hope focusing on explaining everything will help me stay coherent this close to him. So I proceed to show him everything in the room, including a brief description of the sterilization process we use, before suggesting we go to the standard supply closet.

"Yes, excellent, let's," he replies, tapping a finger to the side of his jaw. "But just one quick thing."

I pause, looking up at him expectantly. "Yes?"

"For the record … I'm only thirty-two," he says, as a blush creeps up his neck.

I suck my lips into my mouth to stop myself from smiling, and my stomach does another little flip-flop. Breathe, Sasha, just breathe. He ducks his head self-consciously.

"Duly noted, Dr. Thompson," I reply, looking away to hide my blush.

He looks up sheepishly. "After you, then, Nurse Suvorin," he replies with a stern tone and a mock-serious expression to match.

I'm usually a hard nut to crack, but that does it, and I can't help laughing. I gesture for him to follow as I continue his tour.

Not long after, we part ways, as he's off to another consultation, this time with Dr. MacDougall. And Becca is waiting at the nurses' station, obviously bursting to know what happened.

"You're dead, Dillon," I say. "How could you leave me like that?"

She pushes up on the balls of her feet and wrings her hands together. "I know, I'm sorry. I panicked. But it looks like you did just fine." She gives me a pleading look, inviting me to spill every detail.

"Only because he's such a gentleman," I insist. "But I'm still humiliated. God, I can't believe he *heard* that." I swipe a hand over my eyes, not wanting to go full meltdown in case he happens by again. "We need to seriously can it with the personal talk at work."

"Aw, man. Does that mean you're not going to tell me more?" Becca pouts.

"Later," I insist, watching as one of my least favorite medical assistants, Lacey Petersen, heads towards us. Becca catches sight of her and nods understandingly.

"Gotcha. Drinks after work?"

"Dinner. You can drink if you want, but I'm going to need to eat. I've got a packed schedule this afternoon and I have to study later."

"Fine, fine," she agrees. She waits a moment for Lacey to drop off some paperwork and walk away. "But come on, just give me *one* detail before you go."

I'm not normally one for gossip. But remembering the sparkle in his eyes when he was looking down at me in the sterilization room has me hard-pressed to keep from smiling. I inhale and close my eyes, letting myself sink into that moment. Allowing myself just a bit of hope before I squirrel it all away inside, never again to see the light of day.

"He wanted me to know, for the record, that he's thirty-two."

Becca squeals as quietly as she can manage. "He likes you," she whispers gleefully.

"I think he was just trying to make me feel better. You wanted a detail, now you've got one. Don't make a thing of it." I shoot her a firm look before returning to my rounds. But as soon as my back is turned, the façade melts, and I allow myself my own gleeful grin. Though I almost immediately chastise myself for it. *No, Sasha. Strictly off limits.* And I keep repeating it in my head every time my thoughts drift where they shouldn't that afternoon. Eventually I lose track of how many times.

etween my remaining shifts that week, class on Tuesday and Thursday nights, and studying, by the end of the week I'm beyond exhausted and thankful that I have Friday and Saturday off to recuperate and catch up with homework.

It doesn't stop Becca from texting to make sure I'll be joining them all for happy hour after work on Friday. I ask her who "them all" is and she's strangely evasive. And I kind of suspect she's going to try to get me to go after Dr. Thompson again. So while I'd normally avoid hanging out with more than Becca and Jules, as crowds aren't my thing, the idea that

Dr. Thompson might be there worms its way in, and I agree to show.

We crossed paths a few more times this week, though only fleetingly, but the heavy eye contact Jules pointed out at our first meeting continued in spades. And at some point I stopped being humiliated about what he'd overheard and started wondering if maybe he was embarrassed because he might be interested.

And I can't get the thought out of my head. Even though I know better. Even though I really don't have time to date right now. Even though I'm pretty sure every other single female medical assistant, nurse, and nurse-practitioner on the unit will probably be there, vying for his attention. So maybe I just get to know him. And hope like hell that I find out something that's a total turnoff.

I purposely don't even dress to impress, swapping out my loungewear for skinny jeans, a red, long-sleeved V-neck tee, and my favorite pair of black low-top Chuck's. I leave my shoulder-length blond hair to fall in its naturally straight way and, as usual, don't bother with makeup. I touch my face a lot and have learned the hard way that habit doesn't work well with anything but maybe a basic lip balm.

It takes me only fifteen minutes to get to the bar, which is unusual for six o'clock on a Friday. So when I show, not that many people have arrived yet.

I find Becca and Jules at a large booth with Lacey and two of the other MAs, Harper and Avery. As I suspected, the female contingent is already strong.

"Hey, babe," Becca greets me, scooting over to make room. Jules shoots me a smile from Becca's other side as I take a seat. Lacey merely gives me side-eye, while Harper and Avery each wave hello.

I wave back. "Hey, guys," I greet them as I slide in next to Becca.

The waiter comes over with another round of drinks and I order a diet soda. I'm definitely not looking to make an ass of myself tonight, so best to stay away from alcohol.

We all make small talk about the gossip of the week. It's not my favorite thing, but it's hospital standard, as it's a good diversion from the stress of the job. Or that's the usual defense for it, anyway. We're soon joined by Zoe and Ethan, two of the other nurses in our unit. I can see the distress on poor Ethan's face as he goes from looking like the cock ruling the hen house to overwhelmed by the estrogen in two minutes flat. You'd think he'd be used to it by now. I simply sit quietly, listening to the banter bouncing around the table and watching him look increasingly bored. So when I see him look past me, his face lighting up, I know what that must mean.

"Ladies, and Ethan, is there room for two more?"

I freeze in place at the unmistakable accent and turn to see Dr. Thompson and Dr. Franklin stopping at our table. Dr. Thompson's eyes meet mine for a second, and I nervously look away.

"Sure, we'll just need to pull up a chair on that side," Jules offers.

The nerves work at my stomach, and I feel a sudden need to flee. Thankfully, Zoe and Ethan had settled on the other side of the booth, so I'm able to step out quickly.

"I need to use the restroom," I mumble. "Be right back."

Becca shoots me a look that I ignore as I bolt down the hallway to the bathrooms. Once I'm done, I stand at the sink, splashing some cold water on my face. Even so, I can still feel the heat in my cheeks. *This is ridiculous, woman up, Sasha*, I think to myself. It's just a bunch of coworkers having drinks. So what if he's attractive? So what if just looking at him makes me want to melt into a puddle of goo? I'm not this easily shaken. I take a deep breath, look myself in the eye in the mirror, and gather my wits.

When I return to the table, Becca and Jules are still on one side, and Harper, Avery, and Lacey are at the back. And on the other side are Dr. Thompson, Zoe, and Ethan, with Dr. Thompson somehow seated at the back of his side next to Lacey. Dr. Franklin sits at a chair on the exposed side of the table, having left the seat I'd vacated open for me.

I slide back in, trying to suppress a frown as I watch Lacey already flirting with Dr. Thompson. She's flipping her dark hair over her shoulder when she lays a hand on his arm with a laugh as the waiter returns. And this time I opt for alcohol to take the edge off, swearing to myself that I won't go overboard.

I end up talking mostly to Dr. Franklin, who's actually a really nice guy. In his forties, with a wife and two adorable little girls, he tells me funny stories about them and also asks me how things are going with work and school. I do my best not to pay attention to the conversation happening in the opposite corner of the booth, but I'm not sure how successful I am. This evening is definitely not turning out how I thought it would.

As the place gets busier, and after both Dr. Franklin and Zoe head out to get home to their families, I realize it has been a while since the waiter has been around, and I'm impatient for another drink.

"I'm going to the bar, anyone need anything?" I ask. Becca, Ethan, and Dr. Thompson each ask for another beer, and I don't miss that Dr. Thompson barely stops talking to Lacey long enough to do so. I manage to contain my reaction until I step away, but once I do I let loose a huge eye roll. The wait at the bar is a welcome reprieve from forced socialization and watching Lacey sink her claws into the new man meat. I try not to let jealousy bubble up in me. He's not mine, what is there to be jealous of? When I'm finally able to place the order for the three beers and a mixer for me, I sink against the counter, deflated.

For about two seconds when I *feel* it. Dr. Thompson slides up next to me, leaning with his back against the counter.

"Thought you might need a hand," he offers, looking down at me with a smile. My insides flutter, but now it's tainted with the recent memory of him flirting with someone else.

So I give him a tight-lipped smile in return. "Thank you, but I've got it. Feel free to go back to your conversation."

He does the thing where he rolls his bottom lip into his mouth again, and I have to look away. Why does he have to be so sexy?

"To be completely honest," he says, turning around to face me, "I was glad to have an excuse to break away. Ms. Petersen seems pleasant enough, but I'd actually hoped I'd get to talk to you a bit more."

I look up at him skeptically. Lacey is

gorgeous. Stick thin, with big boobs. Though to be fair, I suspect they might be fake. In any case, with her overdone makeup, tight clothes, and clear willingness to give it up, she's every man's fantasy.

He gives me a sly smile in response to my expression. "You don't like her," he teases.

I shrug, unwilling to outright admit it, and he laughs.

"That's okay, you don't have to own to it. The prettiest girls always dislike each other," he says matter-of-factly.

I feel my cheeks heat, both flattered that he thinks I'm pretty but irritated that he obviously thinks Lacey is too. Even though I know she is. God, this guy messes with my head.

Finally, the damn bartender hands over the drinks, and Dr. Thompson grabs all three beers, leaving me with only mine.

"Becca and Julianna are beautiful, and they're two of my best friends," I finally reply.

"Yes, they are," he agrees as we pick our way around the tables to get back to the booth.

"But they don't hold a candle to you." He gives me a wink just as we arrive back at the table, then starts handing out the beers. He slides back into the booth next to Ethan, who happily scoots toward Lacey. Dr. Thompson pats the seat next to him. It only takes one look at Becca to see the glee on her face at his gesture. Obviously, she won't mind if I move seats.

Lacey, however, doesn't even try to hide how annoyed she is as I sit next to Dr. Thompson, and she immediately goes about totally ignoring Ethan in favor of Avery. The gesture really irritates me, because Ethan is an absolute sweetheart.

"Hey, Ethan," I say, leaning forward. "How'd that performance review go?" He'd been on vacation during our beginning-of-the-year performance evaluations, and I know he was nervous that he'd pissed MacDougall off. Er, more than usual. The man's honestly a ticking time bomb waiting for any one of us to displease him.

Dr. Thompson leans back into the booth, allowing Ethan to look over at me in relief. "Actually great, thanks for asking. I thought I was toast after misplacing that blood sample last month."

I wave a hand dismissively. "It happens to everyone. And MacDougall was just in an especially bad mood. But I'm glad it didn't affect your review."

Ethan huffs a laugh. "Yeah, me too. Not that it's going to mean I get a raise or anything."

Dr. Thompson arches an eyebrow. "Nurses don't get pay increases?" he asks sharply.

I shrug. "Not this year. Budget issues." I purse my lips together, keeping back a snarky response about them still being able to hire a new doctor. But it's not his fault, and I obviously don't need to point it out anyway, as he clearly looks troubled.

Jules looks over, having caught that part of our conversation, and shakes her head. "Please don't get me started," she grumbles. Jules rarely complains, and I know how she hates discussing hospital politics, so I immediately try to switch the topic.

"So how was your first week, Dr. Thompson?" I ask. Jules goes back to her conversation with Harper and Becca, and Avery chooses that moment to rope Ethan into her conversation with Lacey.

"All around, it went well," he replies, turning toward me. "I think I might actually start being useful soon, as I've learned quite a lot." He leans in and lowers his voice. "But please, call me Cal."

My heart skips a beat as I look up into his eyes.

"Are you always so informal with the nursing staff?" I tease slyly.

His lips curl at the corners in a half-smile. "Never, actually," he admits quietly.

"I find that hard to believe," I murmur. Though I recall he did refer to Lacey earlier as "Ms. Petersen."

"I guess you'll just have to get to know me, then." His gaze holds a challenge. One I can't decide if I should accept or not.

"Of course. I make it a point to be on good terms with all of the doctors in our unit." I give him back a look that says, *I can do this dance all night, buddy.* Even though I can't. And if I was forced to, I can't honestly say I wouldn't give in to his advances. Damn this man.

His mouth pulls into a full-on smile at that. "Even the ones who are your type?"

I wrinkle my nose, annoyed that he knows that. "That's not pretending like you never heard that," I point out, trying to keep from blushing. "But yes, even the ones who are my type. As you clearly also do with nurses." I nod toward Lacey, who is obviously watching us out of the corner of her eye.

"Mmm, except she's not my type," he replies in a low voice, without even turning toward her. His implication is obvious, and a part of me does a little happy dance. But the professional in me squirms.

"Probably for the best. Dating coworkers is messy, at best."

"Ah, but not against the rules." His eyes dance with mischief. "I checked."

"I doubt that was the wisest use of your time in your first week on the job."

He laughs and shakes his head. "You're a tough one, Ms. Suvorin."

With a satisfied smirk, I lean in and lower my voice. "Please, call me Sasha."

He laughs quietly. "That's ace," he says, leaning back into the booth once more. But the expression on his face is puzzled. I'm happy not to be easy prey for him. I'm still very much of two minds where he's concerned, so it's best if I keep him guessing. For now, at least. "I do have one question, though."

"What's that?"

"Have we met before?"

My eyes go wide and my heart pounds in my chest. "Why do you ask?" I counter, dodging his question. Could he actually be who I thought he was?

"Your reaction when you saw me in the conference room suggested recognition," he explains, and I deflate.

"You don't miss a trick," I admit. "Yes, I did think I knew you. But once you started talking I realized that you weren't who I'd thought you were."

He takes a sip of beer, thinking that over. "Who did you think I was?"

I take a drink of my own cocktail, deciding how to answer him. "Nobody important," I finally reply.

From across the table, I hear Becca scoff. I look up and quickly gather that she'd been listening to our whole conversation. She goes pink when she realizes she's been caught, a rarity as it takes a whole hell of a lot to embarrass her.

"I think your friend disagrees," Dr. Thompson says with an amused look.

"I just … choked on my beer," Becca squeaks unconvincingly.

"I think that's my cue to leave," I grumble, attempting to slide out of the booth. But Dr. Thompson catches me by the hand.

"So soon? You haven't even finished your drink," he says.

I look over to find Becca and Jules staring at me in a silent plea to stay. Between the three of them, I'm hard pressed to just bail. And with his hand on mine, his strong fingers sending warm sparks over my skin, it'd take a Herculean effort to resist.

"Fine," I allow, settling back in the booth. "I guess I can finish my drink. So long as we change the subject."

Dr. Thompson gives my hand a final squeeze before letting go. "Fair enough," he agrees.

This time I draw Becca and Jules into the

conversation to keep it from going anywhere heavy or flirty. But for the rest of the evening, I can feel the warmth emanating from him as he sits mere inches away. I'm also wrapped in his scent, a mixture of soap and what I can only describe as "hospital." It's oddly appealing. And the thought of accidentally grazing hands again keeps me on edge until we all head home.

It's not until I've climbed in bed that I admit to myself I enjoyed the feeling.

4

I spend the better part of the following week alternating between avoiding Dr. Thompson and hoping to see him. My indecisiveness is starting to wear on me, and I wish I could just forget about him already. But that's difficult to do when I don't know what exam room he'll pop out of or what corner he'll come around at any given moment. Though I'm definitely leaning toward forgetting. I mean, what kind of man is he to take a job and immediately start hitting on his coworkers?

At least, that's what I keep trying to convince myself. But it gets harder and harder as I see him around, interacting with people, even Lacey, and being nothing but professional. While simultaneously rocketing my hormones to high alert every time I see him. Unfortunately, the whole thing has me more distracted than I'd like, and I keep having to recapture screens on the echo I'm performing because of it. My patient is getting understandably twitchy too, and that doesn't bode well. This particular gentleman has made inappropriate comments in the past, so I'm loathe to take longer than necessary in case he gets any other ideas. I shake myself and refocus.

"How's it looking, sweetheart?" Mr. Bowen asks, craning to look at the screen just behind his line of vision.

I put my hand to his shoulder. "Just try to stay still, and I'll be done as soon as I can."

"Why don't you put that hand a little lower, darlin', and I promise *I'll* be done soon," he says with a leering grin.

Repulsed, I immediately remove the transducer I have pressed against his chest and set it down, stepping away.

"You need to refrain from inappropriate

comments if I'm going to continue," I tell him sternly.

"Ah, come on, I was just joking," he replies with a frown. I raise an eyebrow expectantly. "All right, all right. I promise I won't say anything else." He gives me another smile that's no less creepy.

Reluctantly, I pick the transducer back up and move it to his ribs to take translateral images, which means I don't have to hover over him. At least, for a minute. But as soon as I go back to chest images, I feel a hand squeeze my backside — hard.

"Mr. Bowen," I snap, jumping back, my chest constricting at the unwanted contact.

He cackles. "What? I didn't say anything this time," he responds.

I set the wand back down and lock the computer.

"Please stay here. I'm going to get someone else to come finish your echocardio-gram," I reply tightly. I leave as calmly as I can. But as soon as I close the door behind me, tears of anger flow down my cheeks. I round the corner to the nurses' station.

This time Lacey is manning it and she

gives me a harsh look up and down as I wipe the moisture from my cheeks.

"Where is Julianna?" I ask shortly.

Lacey crosses her arms over her chest. "She's with a patient."

I sigh deeply. "Do we have a male nurse available to finish an echo?"

She shakes her head. "There's only one on duty at the moment, Mark, and he just started a stress test."

"Okay, please tell Julianna I need to speak with her as soon as you see her. And I need a man capable of performing an echo ASAP."

"You should probably just finish it yourself," she replies unkindly. "Whatever happened couldn't have been that bad."

I'm about to give her a piece of my mind when Dr. Thompson comes out of an exam room down the hall. I'm actually glad to see him, grateful for the buffer between me and the dumb bitch behind the counter who seems to think a patient sexually harassing me is no big deal.

"Please just have Mark deal with the patient in room twelve when he's done, okay? I don't care how long he has to wait," I insist, turning away from Dr. Thompson and trying to discreetly finish wiping my eyes.

"Mark has another patient right after that," she argues. "It'll throw off our whole afternoon."

"I'm free for a moment. What do you need?" Dr. Thompson asks as he gets to the counter. He hands Lacey the patient file in his hands.

I sniff and turn, but when he sees my face, his expression darkens.

"Ms. Petersen, is exam four still available?" he asks in a clipped tone.

"Yes, doctor." She looks nervously between us.

Dr. Thompson gestures for me to follow him into the room just down the hall from the nurses' station and closes the door behind me.

"Tell me what happened," he instructs tersely, fists clenched at his sides as he leans against the counter. His tension is palpable in the ticking of his jaw and the firmness with which he crosses his arms over his muscled chest.

Avoiding his gaze, I relay exactly what went down, word for word, with as little embellishment and emotion as possible. I leave out Lacey's borderline insubordination. I'm not the kind of person to throw someone else under the bus, even if she is. But when I finish, another wave of anger washes over me, and I start to cry again. Not for the first time, I hate that this is how I respond when I'm angry, and I furiously wipe at my eyes.

"I'm sorry," I tell him. "I'm just mad. He's made comments before, but he's never groped me. I'm just sick of these old men thinking they can get away with this shit." I look up at the ceiling and take a deep breath before I look back at him.

"Did you report his previous comments?" His voice is sterner than I've heard it yet, and I wonder if he's going to reprimand me for stopping the appointment like any of the other doctors would. But what I've seen of him so far gives me hope, so I decide to be honest.

I shake my head. "No. It's a daily occurrence around here. I've reported before, but nothing ever comes of it, so I just stopped."

He shakes his head angrily. "But you've been touched inappropriately before?"

I nod and he scrubs a hand over his beard, clearly agitated.

"How often?"

I shake my head again, not trusting myself to speak, or upset him further.

"Daily?" he presses.

I sniff and look at the wall. "Not that often. Once or twice a week, maybe."

I glance back at Dr. Thompson and he's staring down at the floor, the muscle in his jaw now ticking furiously.

"I'll take care of Mr. Bowen," he says lowly, with a chilling note of authority in his voice. "Please go document this — everything you've told me — and send it to Ms. Magnusson, myself, and Dr. MacDougall. Understood?"

My eyes widen at the instruction, and my stomach drops. This wasn't what I wanted. There's a reason we don't report these things more. Unless it's undisputable, which it almost never is, it nearly always blows up in the victim's face, whether that's management's intention or not.

"Hey," he says, softening his tone and taking a tentative step toward me to take my hand. "I promise, it'll be all right. I'm going to take care of this. But I need you to trust me and do as I ask, okay?"

The reassurance of his grip calms me considerably, and I have to fight the urge to wallow in that for too long. "Okay," I whisper.

"Take a minute to collect yourself. I'll come see you when I'm done."

"He's in room twelve," I offer.

Dr. Thompson nods and quickly leaves. I take a moment to do exactly as he suggested by washing my hands, splashing some water on my face, and having a quick drink. When I head back to the nurses' station, I'm considerably calmer as I take a seat at one of the computers to write down everything that happened. Lacey thankfully keeps her big fat fucking mouth shut while I work.

After I'm done, I start catching up on paperwork. About twenty minutes after he'd left me, I see Dr. Thompson heading back to the nurses' station with another chart in hand, and Mr. Bowen in tow, looking none too comfortable.

"Nurse Suvorin," Dr. Thompson says as

they approach, handing me the chart. "Mr. Bowen has something he'd like to say."

Mr. Bowen dips his head down onto his double chin, looking like a child that's just been scolded.

"I'm sorry for my inappropriate comments and behavior. It will not happen again," he says robotically.

I dig deep to suppress a snort of disbelief, opting instead to tersely say, "I accept your apology."

Mr. Bowen looks up at Dr. Thompson, who nods. And I've never seen anyone scurry off the ward so fast.

"Wanker," Dr. Thompson mutters at Mr. Bowen's retreating back.

I can't help sharing an incredulous look with Lacey before we both burst into laughter. But as the laughter dies down, fear grips me at what I may have just started. Dr. Thompson must see it on my face.

"You should both know that I'm not accustomed to tolerating inappropriate behavior by patients toward any of the hospital staff. I'm going to see that this sort of thing is handled properly, and that you are all supported in putting a stop to anything before it can escalate." He pauses and looks at Lacey. "That's a bit of gossip I encourage you to spread around." He gives us both a calm wink before he heads down the hall, presumably back to his office.

Lacey half-stands to lean over the counter and watch him walk away.

"And he has a nice ass too," she mumbles as she sits back down. "There's got to be *something* wrong with him."

I smile vaguely as I return to my paper-work. She has no idea how much I wish I knew what that was. Because right now he's a little *too* appealing on just about every level. As I get back to my work, it occurs to me briefly that Becca is going to be crushed that she missed this. And that, at least, gets a little smile out of me.

WHEN THE SHIT HITS THE FAN, IT REALLY HITS the fan. By the next day, management is inter-viewing every single staff member about patient sexual harassment, with a hospital-wide memo clarifying their zero-tolerance policy and reporting process.

Becca was, as I predicted, ticked that she didn't get to see Dr. Thompson in action, but as we sit the next afternoon catching up on yet more paperwork, I give her the blow-by-blow quietly whenever we're alone at the desk.

"God, could he be any dreamier?" she sighs. "And you're sure you don't want this guy?"

I shoot her a glare. "Why? Thinking about going after him yourself?"

"Guilty," she replies with a grin. "But I don't care what you say. I know you're into him, so I'd never actually do it. Besides, I just heard there's a hot new orderly over in intensive care."

"Of course you did," I reply drily. "And you're right. I'm into him. Even though I really don't want to be." I'm surprised at how good it feels to actually admit it.

"Acceptance is the first step to hot, kinky sex, my dear," she teases.

I scrunch my nose up at her. "What makes you think it would be kinky?" I almost can't believe I'm asking her that question.

She drops her head and gives me a look. "Oh, girl, please, that body of his was made for something special," she says. "I'll bet you fifty bucks right now he's a beast in bed."

I shake my head and laugh. "No bet. It's not going there. I like him. I confess. But that doesn't mean I'm going to do anything about it. And we're going to stop talking about hot, kinky sex right now before one of us gets accused of sexual misconduct in the workplace."

"Yeah, yeah, yeah," she gripes. "Ruin all my fun, why don't you?"

"No fun allowed." We look up at the voice to see Jules approaching. It's the first time I've seen her since I sent the email. She comes around the corner and pulls me into a tight hug. "I'm so sorry about what happened."

I shrug her off. "Thanks, but it wasn't anything unusual. You know how it is. I'm just glad they're taking us seriously now."

"I think we all are," Jules agrees. "And we have you and Dr. Thompson to thank for that."

"It was pretty much just him. He insisted I send that email."

"He told me what happened. He really likes you, Sash. Like, *likes you*, likes you."

I wave a hand. "Doesn't —"

"Matter," Becca finishes with an eye roll. "Yeah, we know." She purses her lips and gives Jules a look. "I just got her to admit that she likes him too."

Jules holds up a hand and they high-five.

"You guys suck. What happened to the first rule of Nurses' Club?" I admonish them. "For shame."

I take a stack of folders I've completed inputting to the file room to put away, leaving them no doubt rolling their eyes at me as I leave.

IF I THOUGHT ADMITTING MY FEELINGS TO myself would make anything easier, I was sorely mistaken. I have Sunday, Monday, and Tuesday off of work, so I use it to study ahead of a class test Tuesday night. Or, attempt to study, as it were. But I can't get Dr. Hottie off my mind. It seems unfair for him to be gorgeous, smart, sexy, and such a good person.

Unfortunately his recent behavior makes me reevaluate my previously negative opinion of his early flirtation. Because he's clearly got strong convictions, so maybe he doesn't just flirt with pretty girls. Maybe he really likes me. The thought simultaneously makes me want to never have to face him again and go to the hospital on my day off so I can get him alone. And do all the things I keep dreaming about doing with him.

Oh, the dreams. Those are another fun new thing since his heroics with Mr. Bowen and the hospital's enforcement — or lack thereof — of sexual harassment policies. Mostly featuring a much different set of events in exam room four.

For what feels like the thousandth time, I shake it off and refocus on the textbooks in front of me.

WHEN I RETURN TO WORK ON WEDNESDAY, I'm feeling damn good. I crushed my test, had my best Dr. Thompson sex dream ever, and woke up with the realization that I've been an idiot. Dr. Thompson … Cal. He's amazing. What's wrong with me? Am I really going to let a non-rule stop me from giving it a go with what might be the perfect man? Not that I have complete say in it, but I'm going to find a way to tell him I've reconsidered my position on dating coworkers.

I imagine Becca will be gleefully chock-full of ideas on how to make that happen. Hopefully, it doesn't involve signs, or public declarations, or anything else embarrassing. I have to draw the line somewhere.

"Shhh, she's here. Close it, close it!"

I come upon the nurses' station to find Becca furiously stabbing the mouse, with Jules hovering over her shoulder.

"Close what?" I ask suspiciously.

"Nothing," Becca replies with an unconvincingly chipper smile. "How'd the test go?"

I decide to let it go. I'm sure I'll get it out of her eventually. "Great, actually. And I realized something this morning."

"Oh?" asks Jules. "What's that?"

"I'm crazy," I reply with a laugh that causes them to exchange worried glances. I snicker with satisfaction. "You were both right about Dr. Thompson … Cal. There's no reason not to give it a shot. Now I just need to figure out how to go about doing that. Who's ready to help?"

I'm grinning right up until the moment they share another glance, this one guilty. And my stomach drops.

"What is it?" I ask.

"You," Becca hisses at Jules. Jules presses her lips together and nods.

"Dr. Thompson had a visitor yesterday," Jules says.

"And?" I press tensely.

"It was a woman. She told us who she was and then identified herself as his …" Becca grimaces, "fiancée." She gestures for me to join her behind the desk. "Once we had her name, we found this."

I practically vault over the partition as she turns the monitor for me to see. Bile rises in the back of my throat as I take in the website on the screen. "Caleb and Rachel" is emblazoned at the top, and underneath it reads, "We're getting married June 20, 2020!"

He's getting married. A little more than four months from now.

My insides freeze, and I go numb.

"I'm so sorry, Sash," Becca whispers.

I shake my head, drawing back into myself on instinct. "Don't be. It's okay, really. This is the universe telling me I was right in the first place." I blink hard to keep tears from forming. "Seriously, I'm glad you found this out before I made a complete ass of myself."

The knowledge starts to sink in, and I look back at his flirtations with even more judgment than I had before. He's getting married. What right does he have to talk to other women like that? It's inexcusable.

My eyes flick back down to the screen, where under their wedding date announcement is a picture and "About the couple" section. She's stunning, almost as tall as he is, with dark hair that falls in perfectly styled chunky curls to her slim waist. She actually looks a lot like Lacey, despite his claims that Lacey wasn't his type. So maybe he meant "snarky bitch" wasn't his type.

Reading quickly through the text, I also learn she's a lawyer. Great. So he likes them supermodel gorgeous and genius smart. Turns out I really didn't ever have a shot with this guy anyway. My revulsion grows as I stare at the screen, so I force myself to pull away.

"If it makes you feel better, he didn't seem happy to see her," Jules says softly. "But they went into his office, so that's about all I know. I was with a patient when she left."

My gaze flicks to Becca. "They were in there for almost an hour," she admits. "She looked pretty happy when she left."

I close my eyes and grind my knuckles into my eyelids.

"Okay, stick a fork in me, I'm done," I declare. "From now on, he's just another doctor. Okay?"

"Maybe you should talk to him," Jules suggests.

A sharp laugh escapes me. "About what? I'd already basically told him nothing was ever going to happen between us, subtly though, as he never out-and-out even said he was interested. It was just a little flirting. What am I supposed to do, walk up to him and say, 'Hey, Dr. Thompson! So, turns out I kind of would like to date you after all and I was *just* about to tell you when I found out you're actually getting married. So yeah, what's up with that?'" I shake my head ruefully.

Becca and Jules are both staring past me wide-eyed.

"Oh fuck, he's behind me, isn't he?" I groan.

I turn, but it's not Cal who's behind me. It's Lacey. Like this couldn't get any fucking worse. It would've been better if it was him. Because Lacey's grinning at me like the cat who ate the canary. So not only will Cal hear about it, so will every other person in the unit. Scratch that, the hospital. Fuck, fuck, fuck. When will I learn to stop talking about this shit at work?

To my complete and utter horror, Lacey says not a word, simply dropping her coat and purse behind the desk, grabbing a set of files, and stalking off smugly. Becca, Jules, and I stand silently, watching her until she's gone.

"If you want to go home sick, we'll cover for you," Becca says as she watches Lacey disappear around the corner. She looks up at me apologetically.

"You guys couldn't warn me she was there sooner?" I snap, rubbing my temples.

"She came around the corner just as you were finishing," Jules explains. "It was obvious she was listening to the whole thing. I'm so sorry, Sasha."

"This is great," I say with a sarcastic laugh. "Just great. Whatever. I'm not going to hide. I'm going to do my goddamn job and not give a shit what anyone says. About anything."

Easier said than done. The rest of the day is peppered with knowing looks and snickers behind my back. But Cal is mysteriously missing, until I find out midday that he'd called out to take care of some personal business. Thank fuck.

Because gossipy, judgy nurses I can handle. But I don't know how I'm going to face him. Though I know it has to happen. And soon.

---

5

*A*pparently, I don't have to face Cal as soon as I thought I would. He calls out for the rest of the week, so I end up dealing with the continued talk behind my back, which unfortunately doesn't really let up. It probably won't until everyone has a chance to see us interact and gets their delight at my embarrassment out of their system.

I have Sunday off, so I have lunch with my parents — something that doesn't happen as frequently as I'd like, given my commitments. I tell my mom about everything, and she suggests I strike first and call Cal.

Once I get back to my place, I decide

that's not a half-bad idea, so I text Jules to see if I can get his cell number from the roster. She happily passes it on, and I hope I'm not committing some sort of work violation by using information provided for work-related issues to contact him about something personal.

I practice my spiel a few times before drumming up the courage to just call him and get it over with. But it rings through to voice-mail. I don't know whether to be thankful or more worried that I now have to explain it all at once, with pretty much no preface.

Before I can panic too much, I hear the beep, and it's time to do my thing.

"Hi, Cal, it's Sasha. From the hospital. I'm actually calling you about something personal. I'm so sorry to do this, but I didn't want you to come in unaware tomorrow, or whenever you'll be back." I sigh. "I don't know how to tell you this, so I'm just going to say it. I came in on Wednesday morning having decided to let you know that I thought maybe dating coworkers wasn't such a bad idea after all. Well, dating you, as it were."

Idiot, idiot, idiot. "I know that by itself is a huge assumption, because all you did was flirt a little. I wasn't trying to assume anything. I just … anyway. Turns out, you're getting married though, so yeah. It doesn't matter. There's just been a lot of office gossip since someone overheard me talking about it, and I wanted you to hear the story straight from me. I hope everything's okay on your end. Um … yeah. Bye then."

As soon as I hang up, I'm overwhelmed by the feeling that I just made another huge mistake. I literally crawl under my comforter and beat my fists into the mattress, feeling like a complete moron. At some point I decide what's done is done and get back to studying.

Jules starts texting asking how it went, and I just can't deal, so I shut off my phone completely. Even with it off, it's the toughest battle I've ever fought to concentrate on my homework. Around nine I quit pretending I'm getting anything done and surrender to the comforting blankness of sleep.

On Monday morning, I wake noting that there were no sex dreams. Thank god for that. But dread settles in the pit of my stomach as I get ready for work. I'm not even positive he'll be back today, but either way, I'm not looking forward to what the day has in store.

It doesn't occur to me until I pull into the parking lot at work that I never turned my phone back on. Once I do, there are a good half-dozen text messages from Jules, a couple from Becca, and a voicemail from Cal, timed after ten p.m. With my heart in my throat, I listen to the message.

"Sasha, it's me. I'm so sorry I missed your call. I can't ... I don't want to do this over voicemail. Call me, please?"

That's it. I close my eyes against the tears I feel coming. No crying. I'll find him, let him have his say, then we'll all move on with our lives. Probably not without more gossip, whispers, and heckling, but if that's all it is, I can manage. So long as I haven't made it irrevocably awkward for us to work together, it'll all be okay.

Unsure of my ability to stay cool, I shoot him a text message. *Just got your message.*

I'm in the parking lot at the hospital. Can we meet somewhere and talk?

The three dots come immediately, followed quickly by his reply.

I'm in my office. There's no place here to meet without eyes, so just come see me.

I think about that for a full minute before responding. *Will it get you in trouble?*

Again, the dots start as soon as my message is delivered, then the reply: *Let me worry about that.*

Since I'm a little early, I don't waste that advantage, as the sooner I go, the fewer people I'm likely to encounter.

And I'm not wrong, in fact, seeing nobody else in my unit until I'm safely at Cal's office door. I give a sharp knock.

"Come in."

With a shuddering breath, I slip inside and close the door behind me. He's standing at the windows, rubbing his temples as he looks out.

"Hey," I say, approaching cautiously.

His eyes are soft as he drops his hands and looks over at me. Though he looks stressed out to the max. I start to feel like an asshole for causing that … until I remember he's the one who was flirting while engaged to be married.

"Sasha," he breathes, gesturing for me to join him at the windows. He motions out to the sprawl of buildings, the first light of morning beginning to wash over them. "It's my first office with a view. Can't say I mind."

"Cal, I —"

He shakes his head, cutting me off. "I appreciate that you wanted to warn me, but Julianna had already called and explained," he says, shocking the shit out of me.

"She did what, now?" I ask incredulously.

He steps toward me, now inches away, putting his hands on my shoulders. "Don't be angry with her, she just wanted to help."

"If you already knew, why am I here?" I ask, annoyed, refusing to look up into his face, but unable to step away and break contact.

"So I can explain." His voice is laced with sorrow.

Now I can't help looking up. His face is drawn and tired, but he's every bit as handsome as always, and I dig deep not to let it overwhelm me.

"Explain what? I'm the one who needed to explain. I mean, it's between you and your fiancée whether flirting with other women is a big deal, but otherwise I was the one making assumptions and going someplace I never should have gone in the first place. But don't worry. I'm prepared to keep things strictly professional if you are. I love this job, even with all the crap that comes with it."

"She's not my fiancée," he says plainly, his hands falling back to his sides.

"Your wedding website and her calling you her fiancé would suggest otherwise," I reply slowly, not understanding his meaning.

Cal studies me carefully, then sucks his bottom lip into his mouth for a moment, causing me to look away again. But I'm still rooted to the spot.

"She's the reason I left Los Angeles," he finally admits. "We decided to call off the wedding and take some time apart. She's had a little trouble dealing with that."

"To the point where you just spent the last five days with her?"

He smiles dimly and shakes his head. "That's … not exactly what I was doing."

"But you were in Los Angeles. And you saw her." I glare up at him accusingly.

"Yes," he admits with a sigh. "I was. And I did."

"And it's not over between you two."

"It would seem it's not going to be that easy," he allows. Suddenly his stress makes more sense, and I'm relieved it's not my doing. Well, not completely anyway.

"Well, I hope it works out how you want. And I hope that we can put this behind us and move forward as coworkers."

He stares down at me intently. "Is that what you want?"

I break eye contact for fear of … I don't know what. Instead, I stare at the expanse of his chest. Not that that's much better, as it's a reminder of how gorgeous every damn part of him is with his blue scrubs straining over the muscles of his pecs. It takes me a moment to calm myself enough to reply.

"I don't want drama. And I don't want to get in the middle of a lover's spat. So yes, that's what I want."

"Sasha," he pleads. That one word nearly undoes me. Because in it I can hear the pain of whatever it is that he's going through, and his desire to make me understand. But I already have enough on my plate, and I just can't do this.

"Please don't," I reply, still refusing to look at him. "Last week when I … well, I expected wanting to date someone I work with might be complicated, even if you returned the sentiment. But not like this. This isn't … I've got a lot going on right now."

"As do I," he agrees. "So I respect your position."

"Good," I reply firmly. "So we're in agreement."

"Perhaps. Would you like to hear what I want?"

I close my eyes and give a slight shake of my head. "Will it change anything?" I open my eyes and look up at him. Mistake. He's painfully, heartbreakingly beautiful as he looks down longingly into my eyes.

"I guess I won't know until I've told you," he says simply. "But I don't want to overwhelm you. I can only imagine how the wolves have been treating you while I was away." He gives a faint smile.

"Fine. What you do want?"

His eyes light up at the question, and his heated gaze pins me to the spot. "A good many things. But just one that you need to know about." His hand reaches up, and he strokes a finger down my cheek. "Put simply: You. From the moment I saw you. Even though I knew it would be messy on many levels. Though I'm afraid I haven't behaved entirely honorably. And I do understand where you're coming from. But you should know that I'm not going to give up."

I squeeze my legs together to quell the shaking I feel starting in my knees. "You're awfully vocal about your feelings. I thought the English didn't do that?"

That gets a full-throated laugh from him. "No, we're not known for it, I suppose, are we?" he murmurs, continuing to cup my cheek in his hand. "I can't say I usually am. But then, this is an unusual time in my life."

He stares down at me, and I'm mesmerized. His eyes drift to my lips, and it causes heat to rise from my core, all the way up to my cheeks. And I'd be a liar if I said I didn't want to kiss him right now. I came in here so sure I was going to put him back in the "coworker" box. But now? I'm of two minds again. One wants him to take me on his desk, against the wall, anywhere. Now. The other wants to run and hide.

"So, has it changed anything?" he asks softly, stroking my bottom lip with his thumb.

And the next thing I say takes all of my strength to get out. "That depends. What's left between you and your fiancée?" I ask, hating myself for even wanting to know. For letting the part of me that wants him hope.

"Essentially? Paperwork. We own property together. Whatever was left between us was finished last week, though I'd known for some time that our 'time-out' would be permanent. And now that she can no longer pretend we have a romantic relationship, she's using legal matters to keep me in her snare. It'll be bumpy, but our relationship is, in fact, over." He lets me absorb that for a moment before continuing. "I've never dated a coworker, either, Sasha. This is new territory for me too, in more ways than one."

His explanation should comfort me. Just a few days ago I was so ready to take this chance. And with him looking down at me, clearly ready to kiss me at any moment … my body sways into him at the thought and I hear his breath hitch.

Our eyes meet again, and he lowers his face to mine. Desire and panic war inside me as I feel the heat of his lips near mine, waiting for permission, and I'm forced to make a split-second decision.

I press a hand to his chest and look down, breaking the spell. And cursing myself at the same time.

"I need time to think about all of this. Let's give the gossip some time to die down, and I'll let you know."

But really, I wish I hadn't let him tell me what he wanted. It would be so much easier to pretend I didn't want him despite everything. Putting myself out there has never been my strong suit.

"All right then," he accedes, dropping his hand. "But don't take too long, or I'm going to have to resort to dodgy tactics to win you over."

I look up into his almost-too-casual smirk and give him a small smile in exchange.

"Come, I'll help you make your getaway," he says, slipping his hand in mine and walking me to the door. He pokes his head out and looks both ways down the hall. "Coast is clear." He reluctantly lets me go and I slip out the door.

I give him one last glance over my shoulder, trying to think about anything but how much I want him. I put as much distance between us as fast as I can, but even that doesn't help me forget how it felt to be so close to him … or that he wants me too.

***

WE MAKE IT A POINT TO HAVE PROFESSIONAL, civil conversation every time we cross paths, and within just a few days the gossip, looks, and snickers have died down considerably. But I still decide I should keep my distance, as I'm not sure I really want to start something with him while he's still working through things with his ex.

That is, until I remember how close we came to starting something in his office. The thought sneaks up on me and sends chills down my spine. Even though the rumor mill is always ready to pounce on any little thing, and just a week of being subjected to its machinations has me wondering what it would be like if they got hold of something substantially juicy enough to cause real excitement. I can't help dreading the idea, and it stops me from marching into his office and claiming that kiss.

But as if she could smell it in the air, Becca gets on my case Thursday afternoon to go out for drinks after work, since class was cancelled at the last minute. I told her earlier in the week that I'd talked to Cal and that we were keeping it professional but refused to go into any other details at work. Thankfully, she knows me pretty well, so she knows trying to force answers before I'm ready is a fruitless endeavor. But her patience has clearly worn thin. So naturally, her solution is to get me out of work and ply me with booze.

I only resist a little.

"Look, chica," she says, plunking a martini down in front of me once we've made it to the bar, "I've given you time. Now you've gotta tell me what's going on in that head of yours. The suspense is killing me."

"I don't know if I can, Becks," I reply, drinking deeply.

"Why not?"

"Because if I talk about it, it's real. And then I have to decide what to do."

"What are we deciding?" She takes a prim sip of her Manhattan.

I chuckle at her use of "we." Between that and the small amount of alcohol, I'm loose enough to just tell her. I'm going to have to eventually anyway. But really, it's mostly because I think I'm finally ready to talk. So I don't hold back, and even telling her what happened, I realize what the answer is. But it goes back to fear, in the end.

"Sooooo …" she breathes, and I can tell she's about to lay down some trademark Becca bluntness. "You want him. He wants you. Work bitches be talkin' shit, ex-fiancée be makin' trouble. That about sum it up?"

"Sasha be freakin' out," I add, pointing at myself.

Becca nods and laughs. "All right, all right, at least you can admit it to yourself," she says. "What's the worst case for each negative?"

I blow out a huge breath. "Well, say we date, and things go spectacularly wrong. You know our coworkers are going to make our lives hell for a while. And they'll never let us forget it. Work will become more or less permanently uncomfortable and awkward."

"Can't argue with that," she agrees.

"You're supposed to be making me feel better, not validate the things I'm freaking out over," I grouse.

She shrugs. "I call it like I see it. Keep going."

I pull a face and shake my head. "Oookay. His ex could continue to drag him through the mud, making him miserable and ruining him financially."

"Aight, that's where I'ma call bullshit. The man's a doctor, and they never got married. Girlfriend isn't entitled to his money, and the good lord knows he's going to keep making plenty of that."

"You have a point," I concede. She gestures for me to continue, but this is the worst one, for me at least. "And I'm freaking out because I've never felt this way about someone who might want me back in the same way. What if it doesn't work out? What if it's not what we thought it would be? What if he breaks my heart?"

"Ahhh, there it is, babe," she replies with a smile. "That right there. Yes, that's the worst case, and far outstrips dumbass coworkers and vindictive exes. But consider this: what if he *doesn't* break your heart? What happens then?"

I don't want to admit that she's right, even though I know she is. Because the odds aren't in my favor, and that always makes me uncomfortable. I'm not a risk taker, not by a long shot.

"You just think about that, and when your big sister Becca's worldly wisdom sinks in, you'll get there," she says with a wink, then takes a huge sip of her drink. "Mmm. I'm gonna need another one of these."

"You seem extra saucy tonight," I accuse her, happy to get off the topic of Cal. "What's going on with you?"

A huge grin breaks across her face. "I

finally laid eyes on the new orderly and *dayum,* he's hotter than hot."

"Yeah? Have you talked to him? What's he like?"

"Pfff," she scoffs. "You don't just go up to a guy like that and start talking to him. I'm going to have to strategize on this one, babe. Just give me a little time, and he'll be at my mercy before you know it."

"Well, he must be scorching hot to put you in such a good mood."

"You have no idea. Total bad boy. Tattoos, leather, the works. Beyond yummy."

"He was wearing leather at the hospital?" I ask skeptically.

"He was leaving after his shift wearing a leather jacket," she explains with a lascivious grin that says he's every bit as hot as she's making him out to be.

"Well, I hope that works out for you."

She tilts her head and gives me a loving smile. "I hope things work out for both of us, boo."

Thankfully, we get off the topic and onto other, more frivolous things. Which is better, since we both get a little tipsier than we probably should've on a work night.

But when I go to sleep that night, it's with a peace I haven't felt in a while. And I'm thankful for a good friend like Becca who, even when things are still difficult, can make you feel less alone in the middle of it all.

6

Even though I'm pretty sure about what I'm going to do, the next day I tell Becca I want to sit on it, unable to bring myself to take the leap. But I can tell Becca is ready to march into Cal's office and take care of it for me. To sidestep her interference, I assure her I've got it handled.

I'm totally lying. I don't have it handled. I have to process one final exercise stress test that I had to take over for a tech who went home sick earlier, then I'm going home and hiding under a blanket until I have to be back in to work on Tuesday morning.

But two minutes into the test, everything flies out of my head as I watch the monitor.

"How are you feeling, Mrs. Sampson?" I ask, trying to keep the note of panic out of my voice.

She shoots me a dirty look but doesn't seem to be in pain. "I'm seventy-two and walking on a treadmill with a bunch of crap stuck to my chest. How do you think I feel?" she grouses.

I round the desk. "I'm just going to triple-check that everything's hooked up properly," I tell her. "Are you sure it doesn't hurt? Are you short of breath?"

She lifts her shirt and allows me to verify that everything is, in fact, set up correctly.

"Like I told Dr. Carson, it's just a little pain," she points to her sternum, "here."

I head back to the monitor to confirm what I'm seeing. "Okay, well, I think I need to take care of something on my end. I'm going to stop you for a minute and get someone to help me."

She nods, and I can tell she's starting to have trouble breathing. The blood pressure cuff is showing that her BP is rising steadily despite her slowing down. Not that I ever got her going that fast in the first place. So in addition to her readouts, I'm seriously concerned.

As the treadmill slows to a stop, I don't waste time. I pick up the phone and engage the hospital intercom. "Paging Dr. Swift to cardiac unit exam room fourteen," I call clearly, using the code for the closest doctor to come stat. And then I calmly replace the receiver and help Mrs. Sampson back onto the prep chair.

"Someone will be in shortly to help," I explain, retrieving an aspirin from the small, emergency stash in my pocket. "I need you to chew this. It's not going to taste good, but it's important, okay?"

Mrs. Sampson looks at me with her sharp eyes but does as I ask. "It's bad, isn't it?"

"I'm not sure," I lie. "But something wasn't quite right, so I'd rather be safe than sorry."

She huffs and goes about chewing the aspirin as I start gathering IV supplies. The door opens before I can get far, and Cal enters. Fuck.

"You must be Dr. Swift," Mrs. Sampson

grumbles. Though her tone suggests she knows it was a code.

Cal smiles disarmingly, despite clearly picking up on the tension in the room. "He's occupied at the moment," Cal replies. "I'm Dr. Thompson. Nurse Suvorin?"

"We were conducting a diagnostic exercise stress test," I explain, gesturing for him to join me at the monitor, scrolling back to the first instance of abnormal data. He takes over quickly, scanning through, then meeting up with her present stats. He doesn't bother discussing it with me, so I know it's exactly what I thought it was. Her blood pressure is continuing to climb, so I know we need to act fast.

"Mrs. Sampson, I'm afraid there is some cause for concern. To be on the safe side, we're going to take full precautions and check you in," he tells her. "Once we've done some non-stress diagnostics we'll be able to determine the full extent of what we're looking at."

"Do what you gotta do," she replies with a sigh. "There goes bridge night."

Cal shoots me a look that's halfway between amused and concerned. "Let's start an IV with nitro, get her on oxygen, and set up a full twelve-lead EKG. Complete blood panel, expedited, and I want her in one of our monitoring rooms while we run the workup."

He pokes his head out of the room, and seemingly spots someone, opening the door and gesturing for them to enter. It's Zoe, and he immediately directs her to start the Hep-Lock and get blood, while he gestures for me to follow him out of the room.

We step a few paces away from the door so our voices won't carry.

"Don't stress her. It looks like a near complete blockage on top of arrythmia, and anything could send her into V-fib. Get me her full file immediately and have her call a family member who can make medical decisions for her if needs be. She'll need surgery as soon as possible. Stick close to her until I can get her into an OR for a stent."

"Of course," I say. "I'll go get started."

He gives me a curt nod. "Good catch, Sasha, you've probably saved her life."

I give him a thin smile in return. "We're not out of the woods yet, Cal."

He looks up at the door behind me and

runs a hand through his thick, dark hair. It's the only sign of agitation I've ever seen him show in regard to a patient, and I try not to let it make me worry more than I already am. "No, we're not. I'll see you soon." And then he's off.

I head back into the room, opting to call the nurses' station rather than leave Zoe with partial instructions. After I've called to get a room ready, we work on getting her leads and drip set up, and I send Zoe off to get the mobile bed from whatever will be her room.

As soon as he's gone, Mrs. Sampson gives me a look. "I'm glad Dr. Swift was busy, that Dr. Thompson is pretty easy on the eyes."

I chuckle. "Well, I'm sorry to tell you that your blood pressure is on the high side at the moment, so if he's going to get your heart racing, we may have to get you another doctor," I tease. Well, sort of. Because I'm also kind of serious. I've gone through this enough to keep a decent poker face, and I'm pretty sure she has no clue how close to dying she is right now. And I'm sure as hell not going to tip her off until the danger has passed.

Zoe returns with the bed and a male orderly, and I leave them to get Mrs. Sampson moved and set up in her new room. A glance up at the clock tells me I'm over shift anyway.

I head back to the nurses' station and print off everything Cal will need and take it to his office. The door is open, so I enter timidly. He's sitting at his desk, staring at his screen with one hand over his mouth.

"I'm reviewing the data again. Is that her file?" he asks without looking up.

"It is," I agree, sliding it onto the desk in front of him.

"Thank you. I have her booked in to start within the hour."

"Good. I won't be back until Tuesday, but let me know how it goes."

That gets him to look up, a frown pulling at his mouth. "I'd like it if you stayed."

I press my lips together, unsure of how to respond to that. Surely he doesn't need moral support? I can only imagine he's done this dozens of times, if not more.

"Please?" he asks, dropping his hand to the desk. He really does look miserable, and it tugs at me, despite myself.

"Are you asking as the on-shift cardiac surgeon, or as something else?" I ask.

"I think you know the answer to that," he replies, leaning back in his chair and scrubbing both hands over his face. "I have a bad feeling about this one. Please, Sasha, stay. For me."

"Cal …" I start, but stop abruptly at the pleading look on his face. "I still haven't decided —"

"Bollocks," he interrupts.

My eyebrows fly up. "Excuse me?"

"You've decided, Sasha. But maybe I was wrong about which way."

All I can do is stare at him, confused, and borderline pissed off. "I'm so glad you know my mind better than I do," I reply sarcastically. "Next time I make a decision I'm not aware of, please do be sure to tell me about it." My anger rises as I think about the timing of this conversation. *Now? Really?*

He huffs an unamused laugh and shakes his head. "You decided all right, Sasha. Right around the time you started calling me 'Cal.'" He rises from his chair, closing his laptop and taking it and Mrs. Sampson's file with him.

He stops in front of me, staring down at me, his blue eyes stormy. "I hope you decide to stay. I also hope you realize you've already decided about everything else. And that you don't change your mind."

And then he leaves me alone in his office. Completely fucked in the head. I wander numbly back to the nurses' station to find Becca dutifully working away.

"Becks?"

She looks up. "You look like you're about to vomit," she says bluntly. "What's wrong?"

"Have I been calling Dr. Thompson 'Cal'?"

She snorts. "Yes. You didn't realize?"

"No," I admit, sinking into a chair next to her. "No, I didn't."

Thankfully, Becca keeps her opinions to herself, allowing me to stew in my own thoughts.

Offhand, I can't remember when I started calling him by his first name, but they're both right. I have been. Though the more I think on it, the more I'm sure it was even before he confessed his feelings. Which is when it occurs to me that I'm fairly certain I started doing it when I confessed mine … to myself. When I first let myself admit it out loud. And I didn't stop, even when my mind started to resist giving in again.

Being a nurse, I'm well trained in being careful with the language that I use. Words have power. They can keep someone calm. Or they can freak someone the fuck out when they're in a bad place. They can keep someone at a distance. Or they can bring them close. It's why I resisted when he suggested I call him by his first name. I was keeping him at a distance. But apparently my subconscious has been telling me this whole time that I shouldn't do that.

"Aren't you done with work?" Becca asks, breaking into my reverie.

I look up dully. "Yes."

She looks at me expectantly. "Well … aren't you going to go home, then?"

I catch a laugh before it escapes me, and I end up making a garbled huffing noise. "No. No, I'm not."

That earns me a befuddled look, but I ignore it and work on catching up on the nearly endless pile of paperwork that is both a nurse's bane and pretty much what we spend most of our time doing. Things they tell you in nursing school but that you can never fully understand until you're stuck at a computer all the time. Apparently, sometimes even when you're not supposed to be working.

ONLY AN HOUR LATER, I'M STILL NOT CAUGHT up, and am almost hungry enough to consider cafeteria food when Zoe approaches looking somber.

"Dr. Thompson wants to see you."

"Isn't he supposed to be in surgery?"

She shakes her head and frowns. And my heart drops. *No.* I fly out of my chair.

"Where is he?"

"Downstairs. Post-op in suite three."

I don't even bother with the elevator, walking briskly for the stairs and breathing through my nose while I try to keep calm. I don't fear the worst. Fear is for when you don't know what to expect. And there's only one reason he wouldn't be in surgery right now. Death is a rarity in our unit, but it happens.

I descend as quickly as I can, bursting into the operation theater corridor. Suite three is the first door on my right. I enter without hesitation, veering right into the post-op area. Only to find Cal sitting on the end of the bed, head in his hands, shaking slightly.

"Oh, Cal," I breathe, going to him and wrapping my arms around him.

His arms snake around my back, pulling me close as he buries his face in my shoulder. He stops shaking almost immediately, and I don't hear a peep from him for a full minute.

"They were prepping her for surgery," he says, his voice thick. "She had a massive heart attack despite the drugs, and there was nothing we could do." He looks up at me, his eyes red. "We did it all anyway. But she was just gone. What good am I if I can't even keep a patient from dying in my OR, when I knew exactly what was wrong?" He presses his forehead against my shoulder, diving back into his self-pity.

I remove the surgical cap still covering his hair and throw it on the bed behind him, then run my fingers through his dark hair. I grip it lightly and tilt his head back up. His eyes are red, and so sad it pains me to my core.

"I'm so sorry about what happened. But you're not God," I say firmly. "You don't get to decide who lives and who dies. Did you do everything you could?"

He nods. "Of course."

"Then that's all you can do."

He sniffs deeply. "Why are you better at this than I am?"

"You were already going through a rough time," I remind him. "This kind of thing always hits harder when that happens. I've been where you are. I've been there when patients have died and I was already in a vulnerable state. It's never easy, even under the best of circumstances. But that doesn't make it any more your fault."

"Thank you," he breathes. "You're right. I guess I just needed to hear that."

As he calms, I start to feel a little self-conscious that my fingers are still wrapped in his hair, as I'm wrapped in his arms. I look down, a little fearful as his eyes meet mine and his lips part. I stare at that full, bottom lip of his. And my emotions are running high enough right now too, that kissing that beautiful lip doesn't seem like such a bad idea.

He sucks it into his mouth before the thought can translate to action, and the tight pull at my insides finally causes me to press away. A woman just *died* mere feet away and here I am thinking about kissing him.

"Please don't do that."

He pulls back, looking puzzled.

"Your lip," I explain, pointing. "You pull it into your mouth. It … please don't do that."

He releases it with a dull shake of his head. "It's a recent habit. I apologize, I didn't realize it upset you."

"I'm not upset," I protest. But I don't want to say what I am. "Do you do it on purpose?"

He levels a tired look at me. "I do it to keep myself from kissing you, if you must know."

"How can you even be thinking about kissing at a time like this?" I admonish him. Hypocritically. Thinking about all the times he's done that in my presence.

"Weren't you?" he asks plainly. He shakes his head and stands up. "I'm sorry, I'm not myself at the moment." He goes to move around me, but I stop him with a hand on his chest.

"No, I'm sorry. You're right, I was. And I felt like a total jerk for it, then I made you feel like one. See? I suck at this too." I sigh and rub my eyes with my knuckles.

I feel his hands slide around my wrists, tugging them away from my eyes. He uses a hand to tip my chin up.

"I don't feel like a jerk," he corrects me. "I feel … mortal. This kind of thing always reminds me of how short life really is. How precious."

I close my eyes and nod my agreement with a sigh.

His hands drop from my face and I feel him take a step back. I open my eyes, looking at him quizzically.

"This may be an odd time to suggest this given that I just snotted all over your scrubs," he hedges. "But I think it might be best if we keep things professional in the workplace."

A lump forms in my throat at his words, and I withdraw.

"You're right. I'm sorry, I —"

He holds a hand up. "Let me finish, please, Sasha." With wide eyes and terror in my heart, I nod. "As I was saying, I think we should keep things professional in the workplace. But I want to see you outside of work. I want you to give this a shot. Give us a shot."

The grim but determined look on his face tugs at my heart. Because deep down, I want to give this a shot too. Despite knowing it's likely to blow spectacularly up in my face. Fuck it.

"Okay."

"Okay?" He looks incredulous.

"Okay," I repeat with a nod, much more calmly than I feel.

"Well, then. I suppose that's the last we'll speak of it here. I need to go break the news to Mrs. Sampson's daughter. But I'll call you tomorrow?"

I take a deep breath through my nose as my heart starts to hammer in my chest, thinking about what comes next.

"Sounds like a plan."

My hands are shaking and I can't stop pacing. Even though it's five minutes before Cal said he'd be here, I'm ready and waiting. And a complete nervous wreck.

Between Friday evening's events, agreeing to go out with Cal, and talking to him yesterday to set up a brunch date for today — the earliest I'd agree to meet up — I've had plenty of time and opportunity to change my mind. And believe me, I have. About five thousand times. But I'm back to "go for it." Not that that's any less nerve-racking of a proposition.

I've changed outfits almost as many times as I've changed my mind, finally settling on a cream and gold long-sleeved Mohair-blend minidress with a pair of nude leggings underneath. The dress is silky soft and thick yet casual. It makes me feel confident. Well, usually. Right now I just feel vaguely nauseous.

I haven't even told Becca or Jules about the date. Just so they didn't get their hopes up in the event that it goes spectacularly badly. And, you know, so it doesn't hit the rumor mill sooner than it absolutely has to. It's not that I don't trust them, but the fewer people who know, the less likely that word will get out.

I'm saved from my internal torment by a knock on the door. I open it to see Cal in something besides scrubs and a lab coat for the first time. Wearing black slacks and a white button-front shirt with the sleeves rolled up to the elbow, he looks beyond gorgeous. It doesn't hurt that his top two buttons are undone, giving just the tiniest peek at his toned chest.

We both stand there, staring at each other

for a moment, each clearly in shock. I realize it's the first time he's seen me out of scrubs too, or with my hair and makeup done, for that matter.

"Hey," I finally say.

"You look …" he trails off, clearly at a loss, and I laugh.

"You too."

That gets a smile from him, and he offers a bunch of flowers I didn't even notice he was holding. "These are for you," he says.

I suppress a laugh, determined not to tease him for the obvious statement. Instead I opt for, "Thank you. Would you like to come in while I put these in water?"

He gives me a knowing smirk. "Why do you think men bring beautiful women flowers?"

"I'll take that as a yes," I reply, stepping back to let him in while hiding my blush at his compliment.

After I lead him through to the kitchen and start putting the flowers in water, he wanders the small apartment, looking out the windows to the street below.

"I like your place, it's very cozy. Just one bedroom?" he asks.

I nod, putting the vase on the counter. "Yes. It's simple, but I like it. Have you found a place here yet?"

"I bought a house, also in the neighborhood, but on the other side of the freeway, closer to the hospital," he replies.

I can't help it, my jaw drops. "You've only been here a little over a month and you've already bought a house? How on earth did you manage that?"

Cal chuckles tolerantly, joining me back in the entryway. "I'd been planning this move for a while, Sasha," he explains patiently. "I closed on the house before I moved here."

"Of course you did," I reply, feeling silly. "I guess you're planning to stay a while then?"

He looks down at me, a small smile tugging at his mouth. "I think so," he murmurs. And for a moment I think he's going to kiss me. Butterflies start dancing in my stomach, but he doesn't come any closer. "Shall we?" He gestures to the door.

I'm simultaneously relieved and disappointed. I want to kiss him, but I think I'm going to need more time to prepare. Because if it's bad … well, I don't want to think about that. I just want to enjoy these moments where everything is still full of hope and possibility.

"THAT. WAS. AMAZING." I LEAN BACK IN MY chair and sigh with satisfaction, looking out the window at the clear blue skies and calm water of the marina. "And the view is phenomenal. How have I not been here before?"

"Everyone has their routines. I think sometimes when you're new to a city, you end up looking around more than if you'd lived there your whole life," Cal offers, watching me with an amused look on his face. "In any case, I'm glad you enjoyed it. I didn't think it was possible to have better Mexican food than in Los Angeles, but here we are."

I chuckle softly. "Welcome to San Diego,"

I tease. "I'd say we should walk off those carnitas chilaquiles, but it's a bit cold for that."

Cal's eyebrows shoot up. "If you think this is cold, you'd hate London."

"What makes you think I've never been?" I counter.

A slow smile spreads over his face. "Have you?" he challenges.

I laugh and lean in to rest my arms on the table, giving him a flirty look. "No," I concede, earning a chuckle from him. "But I've always wanted to go. Do you miss it?"

"Sometimes," he admits. "But not right now." He leans in too, returning the flirtation. "I have to admit I didn't have any brilliant plans as to what to do next. But I really don't want to take you home."

"So take me to yours," I reply without thinking about it. I flush at the implication, and race to explain. "I mean, I'd love to see where you live. Since you've seen my place. You can tell a lot about someone from their home."

He gives me a sly smile and pulls his

bottom lip in. Butterflies erupt in my stomach and I point at his mouth.

"You're doing it again," I say quietly.

He cocks an eyebrow and lets his lip loose. "I know." He rises from his chair, extending a hand. "Let's go."

My heart picks up speed as I put my hand in his. After I've risen, he doesn't let go, pulling me close to his side, intertwining his fingers with mine. In fact, he barely lets go the whole way back to his place. The drive is silent and laced with sexual tension, and I'm already wondering what he expects. After all, it is only a first date. Even if I have mentally undressed him many times, I'm not really a have-sex-on-the-first-date kind of girl. But then, I've never been so attracted to someone.

When we pull up to his place, I'm floored. The house itself is set back from the street, with a façade of rough-looking earth-toned bricks. The yard is more like a garden, with beautifully trimmed hedges, flowers of all colors overflowing from the beds, and rows of cypress trees on either side, isolating the property from its neighbors. It's a far cry from my one-bedroom apartment and probably easily cost over a million dollars.

"Wow," I whisper.

"You like it?" he asks with a smile.

"It's stunning," I admit.

He gets out of the car, coming around and opening the door for me. "It was built in the 1920s. It's just as beautiful inside. Come," he says, offering his hand.

I allow him to walk me up the cobblestone pathway, under the brick arch that encloses the small porch, and up to the giant, dark wood door. As he goes to unlock the door, I allow myself to briefly imagine the bachelor pad inside. Since he works so much, I can't imagine it'd be all that furnished. But even so, if the outside is any indicator, it'll probably still be stunning.

But if I was shocked by the outside, I'm knocked over by the inside. Fully furnished and decorated, we enter into the lush, palatial interior that is somehow both warm and intimidating. Not unlike its owner. Cal gives me a brief tour of the main rooms before offering me a drink, which I decline as I'm still full from brunch, before we settle on one of the two, huge leather sofas in the living room.

"How on earth did you manage to accomplish all of this so fast, and with your work schedule?" I ask, sinking into the soft leather.

"I didn't. I paid someone else to do it," he replies with a grin.

I can't help the appalled look that crosses my face. Must be nice to have that kind of money.

"What?" he asks, suddenly self-conscious.

I shake my head, unwilling to spoil what has so far been a fantastic date. "Nothing. This place is … well, it's very you. I can see why you're so happy here." I cross my arms over myself, suddenly feeling very inadequate.

But Cal's having none of it. He tugs my arms away from my chest, gathering my hands in his and looking deeply into my eyes.

"This is all just stuff," he insists. "Well, stuff I've worked hard to get, I suppose. But at the end of the day, it's not what makes me happy."

"Fair enough. So what does make you happy?" I ask, curious.

He sinks into the couch next to me, running a hand lightly up and down my forearm. "Up until now? Work," he says plainly. "I love what I do. It's my main focus. What makes you happy, Sasha?"

"Work as well. I'd say school, but I'd be lying. It's a means to an end."

"To becoming an NP."

"Yes. But why did you say up until now?" I ask, looking up into his eyes, suddenly worried that Mrs. Sampson's death may have had more of an impact on him than I realized.

"Because now, being with you makes me happy," he admits, looking back at me.

"You barely know me," I point out. But as his hand comes to rest on my thigh, and he leans in, close enough that his breath is warm on my face, I realize how little that matters right now. From the moment I saw him, I've been drawn to him. And I realize that this was inevitable.

A smile tugs at his lips. "That doesn't make it any less true," he replies carefully. "It's rare for me. This," he gestures between us, "is rare."

I swallow hard, the proximity to him

reminding me of how true that is. How he affects me in ways I can't control or explain. "It is," I agree softly.

He runs a hand through his hair, tucking his lip into his mouth and a wave of desire tingles through me.

"Are you going to kiss me or what?" I tease. "Because if you keep doing that thing with your —" I'm cut off by his mouth descending hungrily onto mine. His hands slides up my thigh, pulling me into him as his lips tease at mine, his tongue sliding across my lip. I open to him, moving my hands into his hair as the kiss intensifies.

I needn't have worried about it being bad. Sparks shoot through me as our tongues meld, as his hands grip and massage at my thighs and backside. I pull myself into him without thought, needing more. The world melts away for the second time since I first saw him, and all I know is the feel of his mouth on mine, the sexy texture of his rough beard on my face, the pounding of my heart.

When he ends the kiss, he leans his forehead to mine, and we're both breathing heavily.

"Bloody hell," he says on a sigh. "That was so much better than I'd ever imagined."

Unable to respond, I slide a hand down to rest on his chest, where I can feel his heart pounding every bit as hard as mine. His hand finds my chin, and he leans back, tilting my face up to look into his.

"Ever since that first day when I thought you knew me, it left me with the sense that I knew you too," he says, his eyes searching mine. "You feel … I can't even explain it …"

"Familiar," I whisper.

His eyes close for a moment and he nods. "Yes," he agrees.

"You may not have been who I thought, but that didn't change how much you affected me that day either," I admit.

"I know you said that whoever you thought I was was nobody important," he says carefully, "but I can't help feeling like that might not be entirely true."

I pull back a little, uncomfortable at his focusing on that part. "Does it matter?"

Cal scratches at his cheek. "I think it might. Something held you back all this time, and it wasn't the lame 'coworkers' excuse, no offense. I can't help feeling like that bloke might be part of it."

With a sigh, I consider whether he's right.

"In a way, maybe," I allow. "It was someone I came across in my early teens. It wasn't a big thing. It just … it was the first time I *felt* anything for someone, and it was *strong*. So strong I'd never felt like that again with anyone I'd dated, and eventually all of my relationships fizzled out because of it."

"Ah. I see. So you were worried that would happen to us?" he asks.

I look up at him, a little bit afraid to tell him the truth. But I've been holding back long enough. "No. Because I only just felt that again the day we met. I was worried that you wouldn't feel the same. Or maybe I was worried that you would." I huff a dry laugh, not really sure how to explain myself.

"I get it."

I look up in surprise. "Well, then I hope you can explain it to me, because I can't say I fully understand it myself."

He chuckles, leaning in to swipe my hair behind my shoulders, and cupping my jaw in his strong hand. His thumb traces over my cheek as he looks down at me, and it has me slightly dizzy with the desire to kiss him again.

"Giving yourself permission to fall for someone is hard. Well, terrifying, really," he amends. "But sometimes we have to let go of how we think things should go and just let them happen. It's the simplest and most difficult part of giving a relationship a go."

"How do you do it?" I ask. "I mean, especially since you just got out of a serious relationship. Doesn't this freak you out?"

"You'd think it would," he answers with a smile. "But I've never been less 'freaked out' by anything." As if to prove his point, his lips lower to mine again, this time much more gently. Though no less heated. As he kisses me, something in me shifts, and I'm almost overwhelmed with need. It's been so long since I've had any kind of physical connection with anyone, much less one this powerful. And I know I need to be careful.

After a minute, I press away.

"You are too much, Caleb Thompson," I tell him.

"And you are too sexy, Sasha Suvorin."

He pulls me back to him, not allowing me to escape so easily again by wrapping his arms around me and half-dragging me into his lap. This time, his kiss is demanding, his hands roaming more freely. For a moment, I surrender, my own hands exploring the hard planes of his chest, the strength of his arms.

His mouth drops to my neck, his lips and tongue tracing a path that causes heat to flare between my thighs. My nails dig into his back and he moans against my ear.

We continue to make out like teenagers for a bit, until I feel like I might be approaching the point of no return. So I slow down, then stop, opening my eyes to look deeply into his as I settle into his lap, my thigh brushing his unmistakable erection. But that … that's a whole other level. And I'd best be sure I'm really ready for that. So I shift, making sure not to torture him if I don't plan on going there.

"I enjoyed that even more than I thought I would," I admit.

"As did I," he murmurs, giving me a half smile. "I wish I'd done it sooner."

A shiver rolls down my spine, despite

myself. "Sooner than the first date? How's that even possible?"

Cal laughs. "This may be our first official date, but we've been dancing around each other for weeks, Sasha. And I'm not exactly known for my patience."

"Cal, that was amazing, but I'm sorry, I'm just not ready to —"

"Shhh," he interrupts. "I didn't mean I expect anything more from you." He strokes my cheek, looking tenderly into my eyes. "And I didn't intend to do anything at all in that respect today, really. But I can't help how much I want you. I'm not going anywhere, though, okay? You're worth waiting for."

I want to say I'm ready now. Or at least, parts of me do. And if he can get me that turned on with a few kisses and touches, I have to admit I'm dying to see what he can do with the rest of him. About as much as I'm dying to see the actual rest of him. The hard muscles of his body have been evident from touching him over his clothes, but it's just fueled my curiosity.

Unfortunately, my logical brain is screaming at me that there's no rush, and to get to know him more first. And I'm far too attuned to doing what it tells me.

"Good," I finally reply. "Because I'm not going anywhere either."

"Brilliant," he says. "And now that I've got you alone …" He leans in close to whisper in my ear. "I'm going to need the real dirt on everyone we work with."

That gets a huge laugh out of me. "You know I'm the least gossipy nurse in the unit, right?"

He grins and nuzzles into me. "Sure, with everyone else. But I still feel like I'm flying blind here. And you're the only one I really trust."

I pull back, a little more shocked than I probably should be at his revelation. I cup his face in my hands and place a gentle kiss on his lips. "Are you sure you can handle what I know?" I tease.

"Lay it on me, gorgeous," he replies, skimming his hands down my arms.

With an amused huff, I comply, and we spend the rest of the afternoon wrapped in each other's arms, discussing coworkers before he drops me back home so I can study.

With one, final, sultry kiss on my doorstep, he leaves me to it. Alas, it turns out that it's really hard to focus on studying when all you want to think about is the amazing guy you're totally falling for.

$\mathcal{O}$n Monday, pretending like there's nothing going on between Cal and I proves nearly impossible. It takes every ounce of my strength not to kiss him every time I see his gorgeous face. Which, as it happens, is way more often than I realized. We cross paths constantly at the nurses' station, in the halls coming and going from appointments, in the breakroom, you name it.

It's almost as difficult as not telling Becca or Jules what's going on. Which becomes exponentially more difficult when Cal approaches the nurses' station in the afternoon while I'm inputting exam results and hands me a patient file with a folded piece of paper on top.

"Note for you. I'll be in my office if you have any questions." I don't know how he does it, but it sounds perfectly clinical. Not wanting to betray myself, I give him a sharp nod and he walks away.

"What was that all about?" Becca asks, watching his ass as he walks away.

"I don't know, but you're going to get caught staring at the goods if you're not careful," I tease her.

She throws me a sharp look. "I could say the same to you," she replies sweetly.

I wrinkle my nose at her and pick up his note, being careful to read it at an angle that Becca can't see. And it's all I can do to contain my reaction to the three simple words written on the paper: *I need you.*

I take a few subtle breaths to calm my racing heart.

"Okay, I have questions. I'll be back," I say as lightly as possible, being careful to bring the note with me.

"Why do they do that?" Becca muses.

"Couldn't they just stick around for thirty seconds and have a conversation? Ugh."

I shrug, trying not to crack. "Doctors say jump, we say —"

"Go fuck yourself?" Becca offers with an innocent smile.

"I'll be right back," I reply drily. "Try not to tell any of your superiors to go fuck themselves while I'm gone, won't you?"

"Can't make any promises."

I laugh and head down the hall. My nerves ratchet up with every step closer to Cal's office. When I knock, he immediately calls for me to come in.

I step inside, hovering at the threshold, unsure of whether closing the door is a good idea.

"Close the door, please," he says curtly, not looking up from the paperwork he's perusing. And I'm not sure if he's always looked this sexy, or if having experienced his skills first-hand I'm now more easily drawn in, but watching him work definitely does it for me. So I close the door. Against my better judgment, as my hormones override my good sense.

"Thank fuck," he breathes, hopping up and rounding the desk, pulling me roughly into his arms. I go up on my toes to meet his descending mouth, wrapping myself in him. In a frenzy of hands and lips, I take what I've been dying for all day: my Cal fix. God, I'm already so addicted to this man.

When our mouths finally break apart, I look up at him longingly. "Well, so much for keeping it out of the office. I don't know how we're going to do this every day," I admit.

"Me neither," he agrees. "It's been torture watching you sashay around all day with that gorgeous ass of yours."

That gets a grin out of me. "*My* gorgeous ass? You do know we all watch you when you walk away, right?"

"I do," he says, "but you're the only one I *want* looking." He places another gentle kiss on my lips. "I'll probably be here until at least seven, but can I see you tonight?"

"I really shouldn't, I have a quiz tomorrow night that I need to study for," I reply with a frown.

He groans and buries his face in my neck. "Bugger. So Wednesday, then?"

"I think I could make that work," I say with a sly grin.

"Probably best if we go someplace public and have a proper date. I don't trust myself alone with you."

"Me neither," I admit wryly. He gives me a mock offended look. "No, *me*. I don't trust me alone with you either."

Cal chuckles and kisses my cheek. "I was just kidding." He lets me go and retrieves a piece of paper from his desk. "Here's an alibi for you."

I take the paper from him and scan it. It's a simple report request. "How very thorough of you," I tease him. But when I look up to find him giving me the most sexy and suggestive grin I've ever seen, my mouth dries out.

"Oh, I'm very thorough," he says lowly, dipping his head to whisper in my ear. "In everything I do." And with a wink, he goes and reseats himself at his desk. "That'll be all, Nurse Suvorin."

On jelly legs, I return to the nurses' station. I manage to pull off presenting my alibi and going about my business for the rest of my shift. But all I can think about is Cal and how very much I'd like him to show me exactly how thorough he can be.

UNFORTUNATELY, DR. CARSON HAS A FAMILY emergency on Tuesday that forces him to take the rest of the week off. Which means Cal, being the newest and lowest on the totem pole, has to step up to cover for him. Which, in turn, means he's forced to cancel for Wednesday night.

I try not to be disappointed, I really do. But Cal is also almost completely unavailable the rest of the week, even for stolen moments in his office. On one hand, that's probably for the best. On the other hand, every fleeting look we share is laden with all the things we can't say — or do — to each other.

We have a few brief text message exchanges, but between his crazy schedule and my work and school schedules, they're barely above basic conversations. By the end of the week, the magic of our first date has started to wear off, and I'm feeling unsure and awkward.

As I'm sullenly sterilizing instruments at the end of the day on Friday, I'm doing my best to focus when I hear Dr. Franklin call out Cal's name in the hall outside the door. Apparently he was passing by, as they stop and chat idly for a moment, clearly not realizing, or perhaps caring, whether someone is in here. But then, why should they? And it definitely doesn't bother me. Just listening to Cal's voice is calming, as I've heard precious little of it all week. I wonder briefly if it's weird that his voice already has such an effect on me.

"So, stop me if this is inappropriate," I hear Dr. Franklin say. "But I know you're new to town, so I thought you might need someone to show you around. My wife's sister is on the management team for the Padres, and we're all going to their first training game tomorrow. Think you can get away? Tracey's a real stunner, and I think you'd hit it off. And thanks to her job, she's got connections at all the best restaurants and attractions in town."

I freeze in place, my heart taking off at a gallop in my chest. Cal hesitates long enough to make me doubt his response. What man wouldn't want to be set up with a beautiful woman who can get him VIP access to all of San Diego? And it's not like we've had any kind of discussion about being exclusive. It's far too early for that.

"That's kind of you, but I doubt I'd be able to get away," Cal replies.

His lack of turning down the actual setup doesn't make me feel good about his response.

"Well, you could always join us for dinner after," Dr. Franklin offers.

My jaw clenches, and I force myself to keep working. Anything but thinking about how I like Dr. Franklin a little less than I did a few minutes ago. Or about Cal's response.

"I appreciate that, but I'm actually seeing someone."

I freeze again. This time I put down the instrument I was wrapping, realizing it's probably best to stop handling sharp objects right now.

"Oh? Can't say I'm surprised, I guess. All the females in the office were on high alert the moment you started," Dr. Franklin jokes, and I hear a noise that sounds like he just slapped

Cal on the back. I roll my eyes and continue about quietly putting everything away. "Well, the offer stands if you ever change your mind."

"Thanks, but I won't. This one's special," Cal replies. I can practically hear the smile in his voice, and it tugs on something inside of me. My annoyance melts into … is it longing?

"Suit yourself. Anyway, I'm off to wrap things up for the day," Dr. Franklin replies jovially. I hear footsteps head down the hallway. I tuck the unused muslin back in a drawer and head out into the hall.

Only to find Cal still standing there, looking down at a file in his hands. I watch him for a moment, seizing the chance to examine him without him knowing I'm there. He looks tired, his hair and clothes rumpled and worn. But he's still as ridiculously handsome as ever.

"Hey," I call softly, leaning against the doorframe.

His head snaps up, his eyebrows shooting to his hairline as our gazes connect. As he realizes I'd likely just heard every word.

"Eavesdropping?" he teases, sauntering

toward me. He stops a respectable distance away, looking down at me with a smirk.

"I don't know what you're talking about," I reply coyly, looking back up at him. "I was just doing my job."

He chuckles and crosses his arms over his chest. "I see. So you didn't hear anything at all then, I suppose?"

"Oh, I heard plenty," I admit. "And I wouldn't blame you one bit if you wanted to date Tracey the stunner. Hell, if you don't, maybe I will. I do love baseball."

Cal shakes his head and looks down at me with amusement. "Do you really think I would want to date Tracey — or anyone else, for that matter — with you around? Apparently, you didn't listen to everything I said. Everything I've been saying." The intensity of his gaze burns through me, but I don't break eye contact.

"I've heard every word, actually," I murmur.

He leans forward, closing the small gap between us. His smell fills my senses, and my eyes drop to his lips as he tucks the bottom one into his mouth. Butterflies erupt in my stomach.

Until voices from around the corner snap us out of the trance we're in. We jump apart just as Zoe and Ethan appear. Zoe looks up.

"Oh, thank god you haven't gone home yet. We just finished inventory and we're missing a crash cart. Mind helping us find it so we can all get the hell out of here?" she asks me.

My eyes dart to Cal, who simply smiles innocently. "Of course," I reply. "Let's go." I walk away with them, Cal giving me a subtle wink as we proceed to walk in opposite directions.

I SPEND SATURDAY STUDYING, WHILE CAL spends it working. Finally, in the afternoon, he texts that he's going to finish at a reasonable hour and wants to pick me up to have dinner. Short notice? Sure. But I've thought about him too much to play games or pretend that I'm not dying to see him. So I tell him to come by when he's done.

Which was a great plan until, about forty-five minutes later, I have to stop reading a research paper on pathophysiology and run to the bathroom to throw up. And I don't stop throwing up for a while. Once it finally ceases, I meekly rinse my mouth and hands. I've just finished and am rubbing some feeling back into my sore knees when the doorbell rings.

I weakly make my way to the door, slumping against the cool wood. Great. Fever too.

"Cal?" I call through the door.

"It's me," he reassures me. "Everything okay?"

"Noooo," I groan. "I've got some sort of stomach bug. I'm so sorry."

"Sudden, uncontrollable vomiting?" he guesses.

"Yes. How did you know?"

"We had two other staff members go home with it today. Let me in."

"I'm not getting you sick," I protest.

"And I'm not leaving you alone like this."

"What if I don't give you a choice?" I croak.

"Then I'll go to the store, get supplies to take care of you, and sit on your doorstep until you give in," he insists.

I let out a dry chuckle but stop quickly as it shakes my now-volatile stomach. "You're crazy."

"Maybe. But I'm also a doctor. I deal with sick people every day. You're not getting rid of me that easily."

I open the door with an incredulous look to find him leaned against the frame, staring back at me with concern. "Oh please, you deal with old people with angina all day, not people who —" My stomach heaves and I flee, leaving the open door and Cal behind me.

When I finally reemerge, I find Cal rifling through my fridge and cupboards, typing things into his phone. He looks up and quickly puts his phone in his pocket.

"What are you doing, Sasha? You should get in bed," he chastises me as he approaches.

I throw a hand up. "Stay away, I smell like vomit," I warn him.

He smirks down at me, then leans in and kisses my forehead gently.

"You're burning up. You need to rest."

"I'll be fine. You really don't have to do this," I insist. But my traitorous body swoons against the complete exhaustion of having just emptied my stomach several times over.

Without hesitation, Cal scoops me up and carries me to my room. Too weak to protest, I slump against his taut chest. Despite my feeling like death warmed up, being held by him is not unpleasant.

All too soon, he's gently placing me on the soft surface of my bed. I sink into the pillows, unable to fight it anymore. He leaves but returns a moment later with a large pot from the kitchen.

"Stay in bed," he instructs. "You can throw up into that if you need to. The worst of it should pass soon, then we can get some water into you. For now I've got a list of what you're missing, so I'll go to the corner store and come back as quickly as I can. Where are your keys?"

My illness-fogged brain can't make heads or tails of what he thinks I'm missing, but I gesture to the bag on the chair in the corner. "Keys are in my purse," I mumble, rolling onto my side and curling into a ball so I can hold my stomach. I try not to think about how horribly, embarrassingly bad I must look right now. Thankfully, he's gone before I can care too much. And before I start throwing up again.

He returns not twenty minutes later, and I hear him putting things away in the kitchen. While he does, I empty the pot in the bathroom and rinse it in the tub. That's as much as I have energy for, as it happens, so I slump back against the cool tile.

It's how Cal finds me a few minutes later, as I feel the pot gently tugged out of my hands. My eyes open. Apparently, I'd closed them.

I watch Cal set the pot on the counter. He stares down at me, half amused, half … I don't know, annoyed? Worried? It's hard to tell, and I don't feel well enough to care.

"I should shower," I say meekly. "I stink."

Cal shakes his head and slides his strong arms under me. And I'm still too out of it to stop him. He carries me back to the bed, puts me down, then retrieves the pot and sets it next to me.

"Rest. You can shower in the morning. I'm going to wash the hospital off of me. I'll be back."

My muddled brain tries to work out that he's going to be naked mere feet away while I lay here, helpless, but fatigue wins and I black out.

WHEN I COME TO, IT'S DARK, AND MY stomach protests immediately. It's not as urgent of a complaint, but I'm not sure I'm strong enough to get out of bed, so I throw up in the pot that's still next to me. Once I finish, I lean my head on the cool rim and groan.

A weight settles next to me on the bed and a warm hand rubs circles into my back.

I bolt upright to find Cal next to me in the dark.

"You're still here," I say, surprised.

"Of course I'm still here," he says sleepily. "Where else would I be?"

"At home? In your own bed?" I shake my head and sigh, taking in the white T-shirt and sweats he's wearing. "Where'd you get those clothes? And where were you sleeping?"

"Well, you're asking questions in full sentences, so you must be feeling better," he remarks drily. "I already told you, I'm going to take care of you, and I'm staying until you're well. I had a go-bag in my trunk with a change of clothes, and I was sleeping on the couch. Now lie down, and I'll clean this up." He reaches for the pot, but I stop him.

"I have to get up anyway," I grumble. I shuffle out of bed self-consciously, dragging the pot into the bathroom to clean it after I attend to my needs. As I do so, I note he's right. My head hurts, my mouth tastes disgusting, and my stomach is tender, but I think that was the last of it. In any case, nothing is spinning, and I don't feel like my insides are in a vice anymore.

I take a few minutes to brush my teeth, comb out my hair, and peel off the sweater I'd been wearing. By the time I'm done, I'm pretty confident I can ditch the pot, so I bring it into the kitchen and put it in the dishwasher. When I get back to the bedroom, I find Cal, still sitting on my bed in the dim light from the lamp on the nightstand, holding a glass of water.

He offers it as I walk toward him.

"Small sips," he instructs.

I take it with a frown. "Thanks. You didn't need to stay, though." I settle onto the bed and do as he told me, but even a few small sips is enough, and my stomach protests feebly. I set the glass down on the nightstand and turn back to him. "Really, I appreciate it, but you can go home now."

He reaches up and touches my face with the back of his hand. "You're still feverish, Sasha. I think the vomiting may have passed, but you're still weak, and you need rest and care."

"I'm a nurse, I'll manage," I reply stubbornly.

With his hand still at my cheek, he turns it so he's cupping my face. "I'm sure you could. But maybe I just want to take care of you."

Looking into his eyes, I see the sincerity. And it frankly terrifies me. Because I've taken care of myself for so long, and it's so part of my nature to take care of others, that the thought of letting someone take care of me is tough to swallow. No. Scratch that. The thought of him taking care of me, that I *want* him to take care of me, is what's alarming.

"Fine," I say with a sigh. "But only because I'm too weak to fight you."

Cal laughs. "I'll take it." He rises from the bed. "Get some more sleep. I'll be right out there, okay? Call out if you need anything."

He starts to back away, but I grab his hand. "You don't have to. I mean … you can sleep here if you want." I feel the heat creep up my neck.

He looks down at me, and a muscle ticks in his jaw as if he's trying to restrain himself from saying or doing the wrong thing. "Are you sure?"

I shrug, trying to seem more comfortable than I am. Because the thought of him sleeping in bed next to me … but then, the wave of exhaustion that washed over me reminds me that I'm not exactly up for anything more than sleep anyway. "Yeah, I mean, it's just sleeping, right?"

"Okay," he agrees with a small smile.

I slide back down into my spot in the bed as he walks around and gets in on the other side. He looks like he's about to perch himself on the opposite edge, so I gesture for him to get closer. His smile widens and he slides behind me, spooning me with one arm draped carefully over my waist. I sink comfortably into his embrace, letting the sleepiness take over. Even in my sick and weary state, I don't miss how good it feels, how right, to be tucked into him.

"When did you know you wanted to be a doctor?" I ask sleepily.

A low chuckle vibrates through our joined bodies.

"What?" I protest.

"This is just not what I thought we'd be doing the first time I had you in bed at two in the morning," he replies. I rub my thumb over his hand, encouraging him to answer. "Okay. My mother died of heart disease when I was a teenager. The signs were there, but she didn't know to look for them. I wanted to make sure nobody ever had to lose their mother so unnecessarily again."

I swallow hard and look back at him. "I'm so sorry, Cal, I had no idea."

He props his head on his hand and smiles

down at me. "Thank you. But it was a long time ago, and at least something good came of it."

My tired brain fights to form a thought just outside of my ability to grasp. A minute later, I suck in a sharp breath. "Is that why you were so upset about Mrs. Sampson?" I ask softly.

Cal rubs his thumb along the back of my hand. "Yes, I suppose it was, though even I didn't put that together until just now."

I shrug and give his hand a reassuring squeeze. "There are some things our conscious minds don't want to think about. I hope I didn't upset you by making the connection."

"It's hard for me to be upset when I'm close to you like this," he admits, looking down at me intently.

A wave of emotion washes through my exhausted body, and I close my eyes against the prick of tears. I take a deep breath and shove back the tide, unwilling to think too hard about the feelings his words evoked given my current, vulnerable state.

"I'm glad," I whisper. "Ready to sleep?"

He nods, so I reach out and turn off the lamp, plunging us back into darkness. I feel him bury his face in my hair, and his warm lips press a soft kiss to my neck, and it's the last thing I know.

The whole next day, Cal attends to my every need as I feebly perform the basics of showering, eating, and hydrating between solid naps. Being weaker and more wiped out than I'd realized, I spend a good portion of the day sleeping.

In the evening, after Cal has served me homemade chicken soup that my stomach finally accepts, he gathers his things and heads home, needing to get himself ready for the workweek to come.

Once he's gone, and I'm floating back toward sleep once again, I find my thoughts difficult to control. And all I can think about is his tenderness, his gentle insistence on taking care of me, his strength. If I thought I was falling for him before, it was nothing compared to now. Today I was at my most vulnerable and Cal treated me with utter and complete respect and attention. It has not only deepened my respect for him, but it has also made me realize that he's not just everything I thought I wanted; he's also everything I didn't know I needed. A warm tear slips over my cheek as I drift off once more.

I'm tempted to take Monday off, but when I wake I feel strong enough. And I can't do nothing all day unless I'm as sick as I was yesterday. Since I'm not contagious anymore, I see no point in taking a day off anyway. Still, I don't push things too hard, leaning heavily on Becca and Jules to get through the day.

I don't see Cal until the afternoon, when I hand a patient off to him. The tenderness in his eyes nearly undoes me, but we manage to keep it professional. When he hands the patient back to me, he slips me a note. I can't read it until I'm back at the nurses' station later, though. When I do, I almost giggle like a schoolgirl but stop myself just in time.

Do you want to go out with me on Wednesday night (circle one)

Yes

No

Suppressing a grin, I circle "Yes" and fold the note. I grab a stack of papers from his cubby and let Becca know that I'll be right back. She's so busy she barely looks up, thank goodness. Cal isn't in his office, so I leave the papers on his chair, with the folded note right on top. As I return to the nurses' station, he walks by.

"The form you wanted filled out is on your chair," I inform him nonchalantly.

He raises an eyebrow and gets a glint in his eye but otherwise keeps a straight face. "Thank you," he replies simply. "I'll be in my office if anyone needs me."

I don't know if that's code for "meet me in my office," but Becca is now paying attention, watching his ass as he walks away. So I don't chance it, even though I wish I could see the look on his face when he reads the note.

Later that night, though, he texts me another kind of note. This one is a lot sexier. Well, not at first. At first it's just talking about plans for Wednesday. But then Cal jokes about the things he would have rather done Saturday night if I hadn't been sick, and it quickly devolves into what he would really want to do in bed with me at two in the morning.

I don't get as much sleep as I probably should, but I'm feeling fit as a fiddle on Tuesday. So much so that my thoughts are occupied with playing out all of the texted suggestions and other thoughts I've been having about Cal since his nurturing heroics this weekend. Needless to say, the workday is filled with all kinds of tension. I try my best not to stare at him because I'm still not ready to let the cat out of the bag, for so many reasons. I also have to work to ignore my phone during my evening classes, but we have another round of flirty texting while we each get ready for sleep.

By Wednesday, the waiting is pure, unadulterated torture. So when my shift is over, I tear out of there like a bat out of hell, intent on readying myself in the hour and a half or so I'll have until Cal picks me up for our date.

As I take a long, hot shower, I wonder idly if we'll even make it out of the apartment. The sexual tension is now thick, and if we don't do something about that soon, our secret won't keep much longer. At least, that's what I'm telling myself to justify my desperate need to have him naked stat. Funny how much things can change in such a short amount of time when you're being honest about what you want.

So when a knock comes at the door a good twenty minutes early, I'm both surprised and excited. But when I open the door, I get an even bigger surprise.

"Dad? What are you doing here?"

"Hi pumpkin, your mom wanted me to drop this off for you," he replies, holding up a bag. "She made Ptichye moloko cake, your favorite. We figured you could use a pick-me-up while you're studying." He eyes my fitted jeans and lacey white shirt. It's not exactly my usual study attire.

I step back to let him in. "That was sweet, thank you," I reply, suppressing a sigh.

He steps inside and sets the bag down on the tiny table just across from the door. "You're most welcome. How was your quiz?"

"It was fine. But I —" I'm interrupted by another knock. And this one must be Cal. Unless Becca decided to check on me too. "Just a sec, Dad." My father looks at me, a bit bewildered, but shrugs and wanders around the corner into the living room to make himself comfortable.

Opening the door does, in fact, reveal Cal, with an eager expression. And he looks fantastic in a pair of loose jeans and a V-neck white tee. It gives me my first glimpse of his well-muscled upper arms. They're every bit as amazing as I expected they'd be, and I'm momentarily stunned.

"Hello," he says, stepping forward to put those incredible arms around me.

I put a hand to his chest, intending to stop him, forgetting how distracting it is to touch him there. His questioning look snaps me back to reality. "My dad's here," I whisper.

"Okay. Then why don't you introduce me?" he whispers back.

"Are you sure?" I ask, still quietly but no longer whispering. "He just kind of showed up. I don't want to put you on the spot. He's going to ask who you are." I shift nervously from foot to foot. Knowing I'm basically asking Cal to define our relationship right this instant.

He grins at that. "I think I can handle it."

With a nervous huff, I gesture for him to follow me. We find my dad seated on the couch, flipping through one of my textbooks.

"Thinking about becoming a nurse practitioner, Dad?" I tease.

He looks up with a smirk, which quickly falls off his face when he sees Cal. "Ah, you have a visitor. I'm sorry, I didn't know this was a bad time," my dad says.

"It's fine," I assure him. "Dad, this is Caleb Thompson. Cal, this is my dad, Anatoly Suvorin."

Cal extends a hand, which my father accepts. "Mr. Suvorin, *rada poznakomitsya*."

"*Akh, vy govorite po-russki,*" my father replies, clearly enthused.

They continue on in this manner for a few minutes with me looking between them, completely bewildered. Cal never mentioned that he spoke Russian. Though it does explain why he was so interested in my last name when we met.

After a few minutes of banter — and laughter, which made my jaw actually drop, as my dad is never so comfortable with strangers — they shake hands and my father starts to walk toward the door.

"Well, it was nice to see you, pumpkin, but I'd best be going." Still agog at what just happened, not that I'm entirely clear exactly what *did* happen, I see him to the door. "And I like your boyfriend. Seems like a good boy."

"You're only saying that because he speaks Russian," I grumble, not sure I'm entirely happy with what went down. And wondering if it was Cal who called himself my boyfriend, or if that was an assumption on my dad's part.

He pats me on the shoulder. "Any man who speaks Russian and asks my permission to take you on a date is in my good books," he replies with a smile. "We'll see you soon, *da*?" I smirk, as he hasn't used Russian expressions around me since I was little. I can tell he was pleased to be able to speak it again.

"Of course. Tell Mom thanks for the cake."

He gives me one last pat and smile and he's gone. I pick up the bag from the table and take it to the kitchen. Once the cake is in the fridge, I return to the living room, ready for an explanation.

Cal is sitting on the couch in the spot my dad vacated, socked feet up on the matched ottoman.

"I like your dad," he says, patting the cushion next to him.

"And he likes you," I reply, settling down next to him. "You never told me you speak Russian."

"It never came up. I lived there for a couple of years when I was young." He wriggles into the couch sinking back into the cushions. "This is ridiculously comfortable."

I can't help laughing. "Long day?"

"Ugh. The longest. There was the hottest nurse I couldn't stop running into all day. And when I wasn't drooling over her, I couldn't stop thinking about her. And there were some patients, a bunch of paperwork, and all that other crap," he says, waving a hand dismissively.

"I see. And this nurse, does she seem interested in you too? Because I might have to kick her ass."

He laughs and slings an arm around me, pulling me into his lap. "Hey, you," he murmurs, running his thumb across my lip.

"Hey yourself. Now what did you and my dad talk about?"

A mischievous grin spreads across his face. "Don't worry. I told him that we met at work, that I admire you greatly, and I would like to date you. He seemed pretty okay with that."

I stab a finger into his burly chest. "No, you *asked his permission* to date me."

He mock frowns. "Was I not supposed to do that?"

"I'm a grown woman. You don't need his permission."

Cal slides up on the couch. "I don't know how to say this without sounding like an asshole, but he's a Russian man. I needed to ask his permission to date you. I don't care if you're sixteen or sixty, it was the respectful thing to do."

"I thought you only needed to ask for permission to propose, not to date."

He shrugs. "Well, look at it this way: Better safe than sorry. Now. I'm starving. I'd planned to take you to this Italian place I found, but I'm knackered. Fancy ordering in? There's a killer diner down the street that delivers."

"I'm game. I know which one you're referring to, and it's one of my favorites. Know what you want?"

He nods and tells me what to order, and I call it in. Thankfully, they're speedy, and in only about twenty minutes we have a feast of burgers and fries spread out on the ottoman.

We chat about work as we eat, and my quiz, and all sorts of other random stuff. It's not lost on me that it feels like we've been dating far, far longer than we have. I'm usually not comfortable with people I don't know well and conversation is forced, but with Cal it just flows. And by the time we're done eating and have snuggled up on the couch to watch a movie, I'm feeling pretty good about my decision to be with him.

And when he looks down at me mid-movie, his eyes full of fire and mischief, I'm feeling *really* good about my decision. I pull his face down to mine, languishing in the feeling of him next to me as we slowly explore each other's mouths with our tongues and bodies with our hands. Like before, it heats up quickly.

Soon, Cal is pressing into me, laying me back on the couch and hovering over me. As our kisses turn feverish, I grind against him, looking for relief for the ache that has already started building. Though really it's been building for days, possibly weeks, so I shouldn't be surprised.

"You have no idea how much I've thought about doing exactly this all week long," he says into my lips.

I stroke my arms down his back. "Oh, I do. Because I've been thinking about the exact same thing, I promise you."

"Yeah? What exact thing are you thinking about right now?"

I pull my lips into my teeth and inhale sharply. "You touching me," I admit.

"Mmm," he mutters, sliding a hand between my legs and rubbing me through my jeans. "Like this?"

"Yes," I breathe. "But with less clothing."

He slides a hand between us and pops the button of my jeans, slowly lowering the zipper. And I've never realized it before, but it's just about one of the best sounds in the world. I lift my hips so he can peel them off, trembling with anticipation.

"I want you naked, Sasha," he says, pulling me up by my hands.

With a shudder, I lift off my shirt, then unhook my bra. He helps me pull it off, then stares as I lay back down. Totally nude, and totally at his mercy. The look on his face alone could make me come if I'm not careful.

"Fuck, you're beautiful."

"I want you so bad, Cal," I plead.

With a smile, he settles himself between my legs. "Patience, love." He leans in, kisses me lightly on the lips, then moves down to take one of my nipples in his mouth. As his mouth moves to service the other nipple, he drops his hand between my legs to find me wet and ready for him.

He groans into my breast at finding me so turned on and slips his fingers inside me, pumping slowly as he continues to work my nipple. I pull my knees up, urging him to go deeper, and writhing with desire.

When his head drops between my legs, and his tongue flicks against my clit, I'm pretty sure I've gone to heaven.

"Oh, yes, god, yes," I moan.

His tongue flattens against me in response, licking firmly along the hard nub, and one of my legs starts to shake. He stills it with his free hand, continuing his oral and manual assault, slowly pleasuring me.

"Fuck, Sasha, you make the most gorgeous noises," he groans. He removes his hand and licks all the way up my core. His hands press my knees apart, widening me and exposing me fully to his wicked, hot mouth. "Now keep your legs open." He looks up and waits for my acceptance. I can barely nod I'm so worked up.

And this time when he resumes, he holds nothing back. He slips in two fingers, mercilessly curling them and pumping into me as he sucks my clit into his mouth, rolling his tongue in circles as his mouth creates a pull that has me instantly hurtling toward ecstasy.

I don't even have time or the ability to warn him before I clench around him, and my vision explodes with bright, popping lights as the hedonistic pleasure vibrates through my entire body, my bones, out into my extremities in an orgasm so intense I'm rendered incoherent as my moans of "oh god" turn into one loud and unearthly cry.

As I sink back down, Cal covers me with his body, his lips hot on mine, his hands holding my face to his. Because apparently I can't even control my own neck at the moment. I wallow in the feeling of his tongue in my mouth, my mind blissfully blank and helpless against the effect of his touch.

"Sasha," he whispers against my ear.

"Mmmm," I mutter, lolling my head toward him.

His low chuckle meets my ears as I start to drift. "Never mind. Just sleep," he says lowly. The warm comfort of a blanket envelopes me, and his lips meet my neck. It's the last thing I feel before drifting off.

The next thing I know, my phone alarm wakes me up on Thursday morning. And I'm still naked. On my couch. Alone. On the ottoman sits a note. *You were so comfortable and happy, I didn't want to move you to the bed. Which I will be joining you in again soon, just didn't think I should tonight. Miss you already. — Cal x.*

I cover my face with my hands, fully embarrassed. The man comes over, impresses my father, woos me with my favorite takeout, then cuddles me and gives me an amazing orgasm, and what do I do? I fall asleep. God, I feel so stupid.

Unfortunately, I don't have time to

wallow, and I rush to get ready for work. My mortification starts to fade as my mind drifts to all the goodness of last night. Being close to him. Talking with him like we've known each other forever. His hands on me. Other parts of him on me. I stuff the last one down, knowing I'm going to have to have my game face on at work if we're going to keep this from our coworkers. And thinking about him doing the things he did … well, that's definitely not going to help. Nor will thinking about his promise to join me in bed. For more than just sleep. Which no longer scares me. In fact, if it doesn't happen soon, I may end up jumping him in his office.

But by the time I get to work, I've flipped back to insecure again. I cringe, shake my head, or facepalm every time I think about him leaving because I fell asleep. After our first sexual encounter. My self-conscious behavior is not lost on Becca.

"You look like I feel," she grumbles.

"Well, thanks," I say sarcastically. "What's got you so grouchy?"

"I just heard from one of the MAs over in intensive care that bad boy hottie has a girlfriend. So I've had better days. Looks like you might be in the same boat. That wouldn't, by any chance, have anything to do with Dr. Thompson, would it?"

I pull a face. "What makes you think it has anything to do with him? Maybe I'm just extra tired," I reply snarkily, lifting my traveling mug to demonstrate.

"Oh, I know you, my dear, and I will get it out of you. But right now coffee sounds like a very good idea. For everyone else's safety." And with that she slips away.

I spend the rest of the day trying to avoid her. But avoiding two people is immensely stressful, and by the time my shift is over I have no desire to go to class. But I do anyway. Because I'm paying for school myself. And fuck if I'm going to miss out on something I'm spending good money on.

<hr>

But on Friday, I'm not so lucky, and Becca finally catches up with me midmorning.

"Don't think I haven't noticed you

avoiding me," she says, sliding into the chair next to me in the breakroom, coffee in hand.

"Just been busy," I lie. "And my break's up, so I should get back to it." I start to rise, but Becca shakes her head.

"Oh, Sasha, you're a horrible liar. I saw you come in here two minutes ago. Sit that adorable ass back down."

I slink back into my chair with a sigh. "I'm sorry, you're right, I've been avoiding you."

"Well, duh," Becca says, rolling her eyes. "What I want to know is *why*. Did I say something to piss you off?"

"No," I protest. "I just … you know sometimes I kind of close ranks. This is one of those times."

Becca sighs, spinning her mug in circles. Finally, she looks up at me, with a wounded air about her. "You know you can talk to me about anything, right? Even if I do get a little cray-cray from time to time, I've got your back."

I reach over and squeeze her hand reassuringly. "I know. And when I'm ready to talk, you'll be the first person to know. I promise."

But part of me wonders how much of this is her still pushing to know if this has anything to do with Cal. On the bright side, that means we've done a passable job of acting normally at work. It could also mean Becca wants to be privy to the gossip first, being as nosy as she is. But I'll choose to give her the benefit of the doubt. She has a big heart, and I know she's mostly looking out for me.

"Good. Now, I know you'll probably say no, but we're doing happy hour tonight. You're welcome to join. Or not. If this has anything to do with Dr. Thompson, he won't be there, I already asked him."

I press my lips together. No, he wouldn't be going, because he's already agreed to make me dinner at his place.

"Thanks, but I need to catch up on studying. Finals are week after next." That's not a lie. And I will be studying most of the weekend. Well, tomorrow at least, since Cal will be working anyway.

"Suit yourself," she says with a shrug, looking defeated. It's *exactly* how she looked yesterday, so it occurs to me that it probably has less to do with me and more to do with the bad boy orderly who apparently has a girl-friend. She must've been more into him than I realized. Like more into him than anyone she has been in a long time, because I can't remember the last time I've seen her so bummed out by something. It's definitely dulled her usual sparkle.

"Hey," I say, catching her eye. "How about we do lunch tomorrow instead? I can take a break."

She sighs. "That's sweet, but I switched shifts with Harper. Thanks, though."

"Okay. Well, I may be doing my thing, but you know I'm always here for you too, right?"

That gets a wan smile at least. "Thanks, boo."

It does little to reassure me, but I decide to leave her be. She'll snap out of it. She always does.

"Aren't you supposed to be cooking?" I tease Cal as he pins me against the island in his kitchen.

"Oh, I've got something cooking all right, it's just not food," he teases back, his lips closing over mine again.

I giggle through our kiss, loving every minute of this. The flirting, the kissing, the lighthearted and lusty part of dating someone. It's sublime.

"I love making you laugh," he murmurs. "You're always so serious at work."

"Mmm," I reply noncommittally. "Not much to laugh about there."

"I also like it when you sound like this …" He slips a hand under my skirt, stroking me through my panties, eliciting a deep moan.

"Ohhh, if you keep doing that, we'll never finish making dinner," I say, sagging into him. Not that I really want him to stop. But he's catered to my pleasure long enough that I'm ready to take matters into my own hands. Literally. I reach down and stroke him through his jeans, for the first time getting a good feel of what promises to be an impressive cock.

"Oh fuck, Sasha, if you keep doing that, I'm going to end up taking you *on* the food, then where will we be?"

"In bed, with lettuce on my back, but still having great sex?" I tease.

"You cheeky little minx," he purrs, kissing me lightly on the nose. "And for the record, it's going to be better than great, you can bet on that."

"Promises, promises," I cluck.

He raises one eyebrow. And it's all the warning I get before he scoops me up, tosses me over his shoulder, and carries me to his bedroom like a caveman. I'd be lying if I said I didn't love it, but I squeal in surprise anyway, which is only rewarded with a low chuckle.

Once we're in his room, he tosses me on the bed, immediately climbing on top of me and claiming my lips with his while he grinds into me. When he releases my mouth, I'm gasping for air but still scrambling to pull his shirt off of him. I've been dreaming of this for weeks, and I need to see this man naked as soon as humanly possible.

But as he removes his shirt, I realize my wildest fantasies had nothing on reality. Lean and sculpted, every muscle in his shoulders, arms, chest, and abs are defined and popping, with smooth grooves between that are begging to be touched. I lean up, running my fingers over them, then repeating the motion with my tongue. He looks down at me, amused, as I worship his muscled body.

My kisses trail down to the waistband of his pants, my hands working quickly to unbutton and unzip them. He continues to watch me, now more alert and focused as I unfurl him from his boxers. All of him. And as hinted at, it's not inconsiderable. A low moan escapes me and I push him back onto the bed, ready to pleasure him. Not that it's going to be a sacrifice. Because damn the man is gorgeous.

I grab the base of his cock in my fist and look up at him. His hands are behind his head, his abs tensed in preparation for the sensations that are about to come. I give him a wicked grin and slowly unleash my tongue on the tip.

His face tenses with the effort it takes to keep watching. So I give him a show that's sure to send his eyes rolling back in his head as I lick down then back up his full length, swirling my tongue around and working his shaft with my hand. It does the trick, and he groans, his head tipping back and his eyes closing. But I'm only getting started.

I unleash on him, same as he did on me, sucking and pumping until he's making the most erogenous noises I've ever heard. His hands drop to the bedspread, gripping it tightly as he struggles to stay still under my provocation.

Abruptly, as if he can't take being the sole focus, he sits up, grabbing my hips and turning them so my backside is toward his head, but at such an angle where he can still watch me. And he slips a hand under my panties, feeling the wetness that's there. It causes me to lose focus as heat creeps up my cheeks while his finger flicks against my clit.

"I'm done playing," he announces, pulling my skirt and panties toward him in one, sharp tug. I roll over, allowing him to remove them completely before sitting back up and tugging off my own shirt and bra. He leans over to the nightstand, retrieving a condom from the drawer and handing it to me.

Heat shoots through me knowing I'm about to have him inside of me, finally, and I can't get the damn thing on him fast enough. Finally, I swing a leg over him, and he guides my hips into place.

Slowly, I sink onto him, letting myself expand around him inch by inch. He watches me with bated breath as I do, and it makes me so wet for him that it's barely a challenge to sink him to the hilt, despite his size. We both groan as soon as he's fully seated in me. I lean forward to kiss him, and the fullness shifts, causing me to shiver with desire.

Looking intently into his eyes, I give him the lightest of kisses before tilting my hips over him. And it feels beyond amazing. I slowly work up my speed, but the sensation proves to be so overwhelming, I start to swoon. He grabs me by the hips, steadying me so he can pump into me from below. The muscles of his abs and chest pull together with each thrust, and it turns me on so much I think I might orgasm on the spot.

As if sensing it, he sits up, hauls me over onto my back, and slides back in. Rearing back, with my hips in his lap, he pumps deeply, and an ache builds inside with tremendous force. But I can't contain it, and before I mean to, the orgasm takes me, I tighten around him, and he groans but keeps up his rhythm. As my muscles begin to relax, he withdraws, turning me on my side and laying down behind me.

For a moment, I think he's going to hold me, as one hand wraps under my head, holding my chest. But he uses his other hand to pull my hips back, then lift my leg. And I feel him slide into me again, this time from behind.

"Holy …" I cry out.

"Too much?" he asks gently.

I shake my head. "Just give me a second," I breathe.

He nods, dropping a kiss on my shoulder. He props my leg up on his hip, then reaches a hand below it, gently stroking my clit in circles. I feel a fresh wave of arousal rip through me, and he starts to move, slowly. The pressure recedes, and it's replaced with pure enjoyment.

"Oh, that's good," I say with a sigh. "Soooo good."

He picks up his speed, and I nod encouragingly. We go back and forth in the same manner until his speed is too much.

"Slower," I plead.

He backs down accordingly but switches to harder thrusts, and my body does not miss that change. I feel the ache immediately, and I gasp.

"Bad?" he checks.

"God, no. That feels — ohhh — that feels so good," I moan.

"You like it hard like that, Sasha?" he asks, thrusting hard and slow. The ache spreads, and all I can do is nod. "God, you feel amazing."

He keeps going, pounding slow and hard, but suddenly his breathing changes, and the hand on my chest grips my breast in a way that spins me teeteringly close to the edge. So when he speeds up, I can't help it, and I come hard as he pounds into me in a frenzy. I hear him groan his release softly into my ear, and it spikes my orgasm again, causing me to cry out as I'm thrown back to my peak.

Finally, I descend, shuddering blissfully around his abating erection. He doesn't pull out but instead sinks into me, wrapping his arm around my waist. I relax into him, and he holds me until our breathing has returned to normal.

"I'll be right back," he murmurs. And then he's pulled out, and pulled away, and the absence of him brings a coolness to my skin that would be welcoming if it didn't mean he'd gone.

Thankfully, he returns quickly, and I feel him slip into position, followed by a trail of kisses down my arm.

"You were right," I say.

I feel him shift, and I turn to look up at him, with his head now propped on his arm.

"About what?" he asks with a curious expression.

"That was way better than great."

His answering grin gives me flutters, and I can't help smiling back.

"I'm glad you enjoyed it," he remarks, dropping another kiss on my shoulder.

"Mmmm, you know what else I'd enjoy? Dinner."

He laughs heartily. "Demanding little thing, aren't you?"

I wriggle against him. "I was promised food."

"Yes, I suppose you were," he admits. But then his mouth drops to my neck, his pelvis tilting into my back as he kisses and rubs into me. "Though that was before I had a taste of you. I'm not sure I'm ready to let you escape."

And even though I'm completely spent, the feel of his hard body, soft lips, and sexy words has my core aching for him again and I groan out a response before I can stop myself. "You make a persuasive argument," I say, panting as his hands slide over me. My stomach chooses that moment to let out an almighty growl.

I feel his low chuckle against my neck, then, sadly, he pulls away. I look over to find him pulling his clothes back on, covering his gorgeous body. With a resigned sigh, I do the same.

A COUPLE OF HOURS LATER, I HAVE NO regrets as I sit with my legs in his lap on his couch. The "fry up," as he called it, was delicious and absolutely hit the spot. But between a tasty meal, a comfy sofa, and our antics from earlier, we're both happy to simply relax and spend the rest of the night talking, kissing, and touching with no particular agenda.

Eventually, Cal nuzzles against me, nodding toward the clock on the opposite wall. "It's getting late."

With a pout, I run a hand down his arm. "That's right, you have to go in tomorrow."

He pulls back, his blue eyes drinking me in in the low light. "Stay."

A small smile pulls at my lips. "Are you asking or telling?"

He smirks and shakes his head, leaning in to kiss me. It's another sweet, playful kiss, and as I melt into him, his strong arms wrap around me.

I thread my fingers through his hair. I'm practically high on him, and I couldn't leave if I wanted to. And since I've got a long weekend of studying ahead of me, I'll happily take as much of him as I can get.

Eventually he stops kissing me long enough to scoop me up, rising from the couch and carrying me off to bed where he throws me into the soft pillows. I squeal with laughter as I land and he plops down next to me.

He finds a shirt for me to wear to bed and we spend far longer than we should laying together and talking. It's comfortable and exciting all at once, and neither of us can seem to get enough of learning about the other, even as our eyes start to droop and yawns start coming more frequently. At some point we admit defeat, and as I fall asleep in his arms, I wish I hadn't resisted him all those weeks. Even though on some level I realize it's because of exactly this; that I knew how much I could feel for this man. That our chemistry both inside the bedroom and out would be like nothing I've ever felt. It both excites me and terrifies me in equal measure. I close my eyes and hope for the best.

11

$\mathcal{I}$'m supposed to be studying. I need to be studying. This degree is everything I've been working toward for the better part of ten years. But all I can think about is Cal. His eyes. His smile. His gorgeous body, and what it can do to me.

It didn't help that I woke up in his bed this morning, albeit alone as he'd already gone to work. But my hair, my clothes, my skin all still smelled like him. All the way home. Through breakfast. And now, I'm sitting here, wallowing in the scent of him on me, and the memories of last night.

I finally realize I'm going to need a shower

and a fresh set of clothes if I'm going to have a real shot at getting anything done today. Unfortunately, that can't do much for what's going on in my head, but once it's done it does help enough for me to start making slow progress.

I inch through the morning, lunch, and part of the afternoon before I cave and pick up my phone to text him, only to find he's already texted me. *Miss you x.*

With a silly grin, I text him back. *Miss you too.*

All progress comes to a screeching halt as I continually check for a response. But it doesn't come. Eventually, I'm able to get back to it, but when I take a break for dinner, I find I'm decidedly pouting.

It makes me want to smack myself. *Really, Sasha? You're letting a guy distract you?* I chide myself. I'm about to have the cake my dad dropped off for dinner when the doorbell rings. I slam the fridge door shut, still grumpy.

Though I'm instantly less so when I open the door to find Cal, still in scrubs, standing on the doorstep. Which ironically annoys me, as I'd just finished beating myself up for letting him sidetrack me.

"Hey," he greets me, looking a little confused at the less-than-thrilled expression on my face. "I texted you that I was coming over. Did you not get it?"

I furrow my brow. "No, I didn't," I reply, stepping back to let him in and pulling my phone out of my pocket. As I go to unlock it, I realize it's on silent. Which is why I didn't see his first text, and now there's another asking if I want to grab some dinner. "Sorry." I give a shrug.

"Everything okay?" he asks, stepping into me and lifting my chin up. He runs his thumb over my cheek and, staring up into his baby blue eyes, I find it impossible to be cross with him. Besides, it's not his fault that he's apparently like crack to me.

"Didn't get much done today," I admit.

He raises an eyebrow. "Me neither."

That gets a small smile out of me. "I guess I could use some dinner. What'd you have in mind?"

He smiles so wide it crinkles the corners

of his eyes, and I melt just a little. "There's a great sushi bar between yours and mine."

Happy that it's not the usual after-work hangout, I nod. "I'm game. Let me just grab my purse."

I get my things and he leads me out and down to his car. We chat idly about his day on the short drive, and I start to relax again for the first time today. Once we've gotten to the restaurant, I find I'm ravenous, and the food does wonders to lift my mood, to the point where the tension has completely drained away and we're back to our normal, comfortable banter.

That is until — as I'm playfully feeding Cal a spicy tuna roll, the last of our meal — Becca and Harper walk in. All four of us freeze, even Cal who is clearly now too stunned even to chew. It's obvious from the looks on their faces that they saw me feeding him. Becca reacts first, and when her expression closes, I know she's furious. I'd led her to believe something bad had happened between Cal and me, and I can see the betrayal in her dark brown eyes. Cal looks between us for a moment, finally finding himself as he quickly chews and swallows and wipes his face with a napkin.

"Ladies," he greets them, as casually as if this happens every day and that our obvious display of affection was in no way strange. "Nice to see you. Would you like to join us?"

I start losing the battle against the heat of embarrassment and guilt creeping up my neck as Harper also looks between Becca and me, then Cal and I, as if completely unsure how to act.

"Thanks, but we don't want to interrupt your date," Becca replies pointedly.

"It's really no trouble," Cal insists, in no way refuting her supposition that this is a date. I mean, of course it is, but he's now basically confirmed it, and Harper looks like she can barely suppress her glee. Hello, rumor mill.

Becca presses her lips together, looking like she's about to explode.

"That's kind of you, but it looks like you're finishing up," Harper interjects, looking askance at Becca. "It'll probably take us a while to figure out what we want anyway, right, Becca? I wasn't even sure I wanted to come here, since I've never had sushi before. But I insisted on treating Becca for picking up my shift today so I could go with my family to see my grandma in hospice." Harper abruptly stops, realizing she's rambling, and smiles nervously.

"Well, I do hope your grandmother is comfortable and being well looked after," Cal replies kindly, though even he's starting to succumb to the awkwardness of this encounter. He shoots me a look, pleading for me to say something.

I clear my throat. "Yes, I hope she's doing okay," I amend, throwing a sympathetic look toward Harper before shifting my gaze to Becca. "Why don't we talk for a minute and give Harper a chance to go look at the menu?"

A sudden sweet and completely dangerous smile breaks over Becca's face. "Yes, let's," she says, venomously cheerful.

Cal squeezes my hand and I look over at him. Pity is written all over his face, as he clearly senses what's about to go down. "I'll be in the car," he murmurs softly before sliding out of the booth and giving Becca a wary smile. "Enjoy your evening."

Becca just shoots him a look as he leaves, folding her arms over her chest. Since she's obviously not going to sit down, I stand up and approach carefully.

"Hey," I say lamely.

"So. How long has this been going on?" she asks sharply.

"Okay, so, we're doing this," I reply with a sigh. "It's been about a week. I'm sorry, Becca, I just wanted to keep it to myself until … I don't know, until I knew where it was going."

She barks a sharp laugh. "So instead you made me think something awful had happened between you two? Right. Just be honest, Sasha, what you really mean is that you wanted to keep it from me because you don't trust me."

"It's not about that," I insist. "You know me, Becks, I'm just a private person. Taking this step was huge for me. I just needed some time."

"Well, you guys looked pretty cozy," she grumbles. I breathe an inward sigh of relief as I feel her anger starting to dissipate. And lo and behold, she turns the puppy dog eyes on.

Now I brace myself for the oncoming guilt trip. "Were you ever going to tell me?"

I shift uncomfortably. "I hadn't thought that far ahead," I admit. "Probably? It's just been nice to be in this little bubble of it being only me and him." I shrug, not sure I can fully explain it. Becca is so different, always telling me everything, usually in far more detail than is necessary.

She just stares at me for a minute, the hurt written all over her face. Her mouth opens and closes a couple of times before she shakes her head. "You probably shouldn't keep him waiting," she finally says, averting her eyes.

My heart sinks into my stomach at the thought of leaving things like this with her. Because even though she's not mad anymore, I know she's still disappointed and that things won't be right with her until she's come to terms with it enough to forgive me. Unfortunately, I'm not very good at explaining myself to others. It just doesn't come naturally. And I know it's going to make getting over this bump in our friendship difficult.

"Becca, I'm sorry, I don't know what else to say," I reply honestly. "I hope you don't stay mad at me forever. Our friendship means a lot to me."

Normally a huge softie, my words don't have any effect on her; if anything, she looks even sadder. "If that were true you would've told me. And you definitely wouldn't have lied to me." She sighs, and a leaden weight settles on my heart. "I'll see you around, Sasha." She turns and heads to the counter to meet back up with Harper.

I stand there for a few moments, gathering the will to leave. I stare after her, hoping for her to turn around with forgiveness in her eyes. But she doesn't.

Eventually, I turn and walk out. I don't even register I've found my way back to the car until I'm sliding into it. Cal looks over at me nervously, his dark hair tousled from running his hands through it. Thankfully, he doesn't say anything, doesn't ask what happened, and definitely doesn't throw me a pity party. He simply takes my hand and drives back to my place.

When he parks in front of my building, I sit there numbly for a moment, unsure of whether I want to be alone to process all of this or invite him upstairs and distract myself from the sting of Becca's reaction.

"So I take it that was Becca finding out about us," he says lightly after several minutes of silence. "And that she wasn't terribly thrilled you hadn't told her."

I nod morosely, examining my hands in my lap. "I kind of … let her believe something bad had happened between us last week," I admit. "So she has good reason to be upset."

"Ah. I see." He stares out the window for a moment. "And I hate to add to things, but I fear this means we've reached a tipping point."

I huff a laugh through my nose. "Meaning?"

He turns to look at me. "Meaning, we can continue seeing one another, knowing our coworkers are all likely to soon know that that's exactly what's happening," he replies, "or if you'd intended to keep this a secret and now that it's not would rather put an end to things …" He looks at me meaningfully. He knows how much that thought scared me.

It sinks in that he's giving me an out. If

I'm really not okay continuing a relationship with our coworkers being all up in our business, I can walk away.

I quickly weigh the options in my mind. Staying together will mean constant gossip, interference, and tension at work. Possibly indefinitely. Even thinking about the drama makes me want to run and hide. But ending things … that thought sends a sharp pain through my gut. Neither option is sunshine and roses. And the idea of giving him up now … I look up at him, tears swimming in my eyes.

"I don't want to end things."

The relief on his face is obvious, and he reaches over to brush a tear from my cheek. He then unclips his seatbelt and gets out, coming around to open my door. He helps me out, then leads me up to my apartment.

As soon as I let us in, he pulls me into his arms. His thumbs stroke my cheeks, his strong hands holding my face. I look up into his eyes, which are now a stormy blue-grey, and I see a swirl of emotion too complex to read. His thick brows are pinched together, his mouth turned down as his eyes search mine. A thumb slides across my lip. He leans in and brushes his mouth over mine tentatively.

I close my eyes and let the tears slip over my cheeks, not caring anymore whether I cry in front of him. Between Becca's disappointment and realizing that Cal and I are truly at a crossroads, the emotion is just too much. I've never handled my feelings well, always pushing them down. But these … well, they're not staying down. I push my lips into his, needing the connection. Needing to forget everything else.

He seems hesitant at first, his lips keeping light contact. But I need more if I'm going to wipe all of this from my mind. I grab his bottom lip with my teeth and wrap my arms around his neck. I push my tongue into his mouth, needing to taste him. Finally, he relents, and he presses me into the wall next to the door, his whole body responding to my invitation.

His hands slip under my shirt, sliding up my back and undoing the clasp of my bra as his hips pin me to the wall. I lift my arms, begging him silently to undress me. With a growl, he pushes off my lips and tears off my shirt and bra together, exposing my breasts to the cool air. His mouth dips down, mercilessly pulling at each nipple in turn. The heat begins to rise in my core, blessedly taking away any thought but him from my mind.

I pull at his shirt until it's joined mine on the floor, running my hands over the muscles of his chest and stomach. My hands slip to his hips, working his scrub bottoms and boxers down until they fall to the floor. He steps out of them impatiently, grabbing at the waistband of my jeans and pulling me into the bedroom behind us.

He pushes me backward onto the bed, climbing quickly after me and tugging off my bottoms. I roll over and scoot to the head of the bed, retrieving a condom from the night-stand. When I turn back, he's sat on the end of the bed on his haunches, staring at me with so much raw passion on his face I can barely stand it. I toss him the condom, which he deftly catches, then I turn around so I'm facing away, and look back at him pointedly, silently saying, *"Take me."* His muscles tense and his cock twitches, growing so hard it makes me beyond ready for him. I turn my head toward the headboard again. I can't handle his intensity any more than I can handle my own right now.

His hand runs over my backside, dipping between my thighs. His fingers slide over my wet core, and he sucks in a sharp breath. I hear the foil packet rip and then a moment later, the hard tip of his cock nudges between my legs.

My hips tilt back reflexively, begging him for it. I need this. I need him. The realization breaks the dam of emotion, and tears slip out of my eyes as he pushes into me. But it doesn't diminish how good he feels buried inside. I tilt forward then push back, starting a rhythm that he quickly picks up. He grabs my hips, reinforcing each thrust.

Tears continue to leak silently from my eyes as we both pant quietly into the pleasure. The loudest sound in the room is the sound of his hips slapping into my backside, flesh meeting flesh: the sound of us. Together as one as we experience the basest of pleasures, as he rides me through this mess of feelings swirling inside of me. The dull ache of my orgasm building begins, and I spasm around him. He wordlessly takes note, slamming harder on each thrust until little gasps escape me every time his cock fills me, with every inch I climb up the peak until I need to bury my face in the bedspread as I cry out my orgasm.

Suddenly, he pushes forward until his knees are at my sides, lowering my hips into his lap so he can go deeper, harder, faster. He takes me like an animal, pounding furiously. As the sheer force and speed of his thrusts register, I'm thrown back over the edge into an oblivion so deep and wide that I lose all sense. He's fucking me so hard that it's starting to hurt, but in a way that only adds to the pleasure. He keeps going, and so does my climax, taking me so deeply, so completely that I'm shaking with the gratification spreading through every cell of my body as he masters me completely.

Finally, unable to hold myself up, my arms collapse underneath me and I sink into the pillow. Only then does he slow and stop, backing off so I can sink fully down to the mattress.

He rolls me gently over, and I'm not

surprised to find him covered in sweat. What I am surprised to see is his huge, hard cock still fully at attention. Unsure if I can take anymore, but unable to speak, I simply shake my head.

He leans forward, his expression veiled, and gives me a light kiss. One that he trails down my body, until his mouth covers my pussy, his tongue oh-so-gently flattened against the throbbing, slightly sore surface. He licks up my core, flicking the tip of his tongue across my clit. I moan quietly in approval. So he does it again, and again, until I can't tell if it's because of his tongue or if it's my own arousal spread all over.

It's then that he climbs over me, one hand gently cupping my face, the other positioning his cock to enter me. But he waits, tip at my entrance, for me to give permission. And with one nod, he slides slowly in, filling my aching core. It straddles the border of pleasure and pain, but as his mouth finds mine, his body covering me completely, I surrender and let him take what he wants. His head drops next to mine, his breathing labored in my ear.

"Stay with me." He says it so quietly I almost don't hear him.

I press my hands to the sides of his face, lifting his head so I can look at him.

"I'm with you," I whisper.

"Completely?"

"Completely," I agree as tears flow afresh out of the corners of my eyes.

With his forehead pressed to mine, his hips tilt rapidly and I feel the orgasm take him in the tightness of his shoulders, the gasping of his breath. And then he stills, sinking down onto me, his head tucked into the crook of my neck. I wrap my legs around him, holding him with my arms until his breathing evens out and his heart rate returns to normal.

Once it does, he climbs off of me, offering me a hand. I take it, unsure of what he intends to do. He leads me into the bathroom, where he turns on the shower and discards the condom. He helps me into the tub enclosure, then joins me, pulling the curtain closed.

Wordlessly, he rinses off under the hot stream of water. I twist my hair up and use the clip on the tub ledge to hold it in place so I can step closer to him and get clean. He's still strangely so quiet, though, through the entire shower and after as we dry off.

"I'm afraid I don't have a change of clothes with me," he admits as I strip the damp comforter off the bed and replace it with a clean, dry blanket.

I throw him a vague smile over my shoulder. "Well, if you want to stay I can throw your scrubs in the wash."

He grabs my wrist, gently tugging me into his arms. "Of course I want to stay."

I smile up at him lightly. "Then I'll go put them in." I press out of his arms but feel a swell of emotion as I turn away. *God, what is wrong with me?*

Shaking myself a little, I retrieve his clothes from the hall, as well as my own, and toss it all into the washing machine.

When I get back to the bedroom, Cal is under the covers, one arm slung behind his head to prop him up. In a word, he's stunning. But I realize all this emotion is because I've chosen him. Which was fine when we were in our bubble. Consciously remaking that choice when I know how hard things are going to be at work because of it is a completely different ballgame. And it's not the drama I'm more scared of, it's how much I already care for him that I'd even make that decision in the first place.

I sit down on the bed next to him, facing him. "Do you think this is going too fast?"

He frowns deeply, drawing himself upright so he's sitting opposite me. "That's a loaded question if I've ever heard one."

I shrug. "You seemed pretty worried that the thing with Becca and Harper would make me change my mind about us."

"I was. I am."

"Even though I've told you twice since then that I'm still in this?"

He gives me a half-hearted smile. "It's easy to do now, as the shit's only starting to hit the fan. Them finding out is just the beginning."

"Yes," I agree. "But it doesn't seem weird to you that we've only been seeing each other for two weeks and we're both ..." I trail off, realizing it might not be fair to lump his feelings with mine. Because maybe I'm misinterpreting things.

"Really into each other?" he offers with a

sideways smile, running his hand along my thigh.

I snort. "That's the mild version, but yes, that's basically where I was going with that."

He reaches up and his fingers now trail down my jaw. "I don't know. One day at a time, love. And this was a particularly intense one."

I take a deep breath, realizing how truly exhausted I am. "Fair enough." I slide down into the bed and Cal slips behind me, wrapping me in his arms. It doesn't take long for me to fall into a blissfully deep and dreamless sleep, despite my worry.

12

When we wake on Sunday, Cal convinces me to let him spend the day with me, despite my need to study. But he thoughtfully accounted for that, agreeing to reward me for my accomplishments with food and *other things*, said with a wink. There's no way on earth I could say no to that. Besides, it's his only day off, and if that's how he wants to spend it, who am I to stop him?

I surprisingly manage to get quite a bit done. The simplicity of the day and the sheer decadence of having Cal wait on me helps me keep my mind off of anything that might worry me. That can all wait.

But as Cal goes to return to his own home and bed for the night so he can get ready for his workweek, I'm reluctant to let him, knowing reality is about to come crashing back in.

I even dream about it. Well, they're borderline nightmares. Even unconscious, my mind flips through all the horrible possibilities that await.

So when I wake up on Monday morning at my normal ungodly hour, I'm even more reluctant than usual to leave the warmth of bed. But I've always been one to put on my big-girl panties and take what's coming. It's the fastest way to get it over with.

When I get to work, I attempt to approach the nurses' station from the opposite direction, hoping to just drop my things off without Becca noticing.

"Morning meeting has been moved back fifteen minutes," she says without turning around. I jump about a foot in the air, not having expected her to notice me, much less say something.

"Okay, thanks," I mumble, glad for the extra time to go refill my travel mug. But before I can get far, Becca actually turns toward me.

"For the record, I'm not going to tell anybody. Not even Jules. Since you obviously don't trust me, I just wanted you to know."

My insides twinge with guilt. "Becks —"

"Don't call me that," she snaps.

And I can't help it, that really pisses me off. "Oh, no. *You* don't," I demand. "I screwed up. I'm sorry, okay? Either forgive me so we can move on, or don't. I can't make you. But just remember that you're not a fucking saint either, Becca, and I've put up with a lot of shit from you over the years. Because that's what friends do." I grip my mug tightly and stomp off to the break room more immaturely than I'd usually allow myself to. I swear, sometimes we're more like sisters than friends the way we get after each other. That thought just makes me even sadder and angrier with the whole situation.

My mood isn't helped when Harper, Avery, and Lacey enter the room, giggling among themselves. They stop once they spot me, give each other looks, and giggle some more. Just great. So Becca learns to keep her trap shut, but Harper's gone and mouthed off already. Awesome.

I shake my head and, without a word to any of them, stalk out of the room. I have a feeling I'm going to be making a lot of dramatic exits today.

I spot Jules talking to Becca at the nurses' station and instinctively move toward them. But I stop myself short, knowing I won't be welcomed by Becca. Unfortunately, Jules spots me before I can change course. Her pitying look tells me she's already heard the news. Well, fuck. This might be a new gossip record. Not even ten minutes into first shift.

"So who'd you hear it from?" I ask blandly as I finish my approach.

Jules looks down the hall both ways before answering. "That part doesn't matter," she says in hushed tones. "What matters is *what* I heard. Were you really awkwardly force-feeding Dr. Thompson in public?"

"Excuse me?" I ask, my eyebrows jumping to my hairline.

Jules looks sheepish. "I didn't think so."

"Spill, Jules."

She takes a deep breath to ready herself but is stopped short as Dr. MacDougall rushes around the corner, heading to the staff meeting room.

"Later," she promises, reaching out to squeeze my hand as others start trickling past toward the morning meeting.

Jules walks with me, not even noticing Becca hasn't joined us. She's going to be all over both of us once she figures out what else is going on. She fancies herself something of a mother figure toward us, so I know that once she finds out, she's not going to let our little tiff go.

The staff meeting is nearly unbearable. Cal comes in after it has already started, and all the looks of amusement I've been getting shift to empathetic looks being thrown his way, and I'm dying to know what else the rumor mill is saying. And strangely, he doesn't look at me once. After the meeting has ended, I realize I'm also getting the talk-behind-your-back treatment from almost the entire staff.

But I don't have time to dwell, as my first appointment has already technically started and I'm late. So I push through it all and focus on work.

By the afternoon I still haven't caught back up with Jules. Unfortunately, as I'm rushing between appointments, I encounter Lacey manning the nurses' station.

"You look like you're ready to go home," she says with fake pity in her voice. Something about it bothers me, in a different way than all the gossip clearly being passed just outside of my hearing.

I breathe in through my nose, determined not to let her get to me. "Nope, I'm great, but thanks." I go back to grabbing the file for the patient I'm supposed to see next.

Her fake tone of concern takes on a distinct edge of mockery. "Are you sure? Because if I went on a date with someone who was telling everyone he only did it out of pity, I'd be pretty upset."

I freeze, looking up from the file in my hand. And I can't help it, I burst into laughter. "*That's* what everyone is saying? Really?" I laugh so hard I have to clutch my stomach and wipe a tear from the corner of my eye. I don't think for one second that Cal said anything of the sort, and that actually warms my heart toward him. Because I can trust him. I know I can. That's why it's so funny, because it couldn't be further from anything that would ever come out of his mouth.

Lacey crosses her arms over her chest, clearly unhappy with my reaction.

"Yes," she snips. "And it's not exactly hard to believe. I mean, why else would a guy like that go out with someone like you?"

Realization dawns on me as I read between the lines. But I can't outright accuse her of starting, or at the very least helping along, that rumor. I simply give her a dangerous smile.

"I guess that would be hard for *someone like you* to understand," I reply smugly. And then I walk away. Once I've gotten around the corner, I chuckle softly to myself and make a mental note to find Cal and clue him in, if he doesn't already know. Strangely, I feel relieved. Because if that's the worst thing they're saying, this might be easier than I thought.

Unfortunately, I don't end up catching up with either Jules or Cal before end of shift, and I can't find either of them anywhere when it's time to head home. Though I'm not particularly worried. After Lacey's revelation, the looks became a whole lot easier to deal with knowing that once people realized it was all a lie, I'd get the last laugh, and in the end it would probably make them back the hell off. All in all, there are worse things that could've happened.

I'm at home eating leftovers and studying when the doorbell rings around eight. I open the door to find Cal.

"Do you ever take your phone off silent?" he teases, leaning in for a kiss.

"I don't know, is this another pity date?" I tease back.

He stops short of my lips, giving me a questioning look. "Pardon?"

"You haven't heard," I realize aloud. I figured when I hadn't caught up with him, he'd probably hear it from someone else eventually. But I guess not. I gesture for him to come in and close the door behind him. Once we've settled on the couch, I tell him what Lacey said. Before I can get any further, he jumps in, clearly upset.

"That's *absurd*," he scoffs in a clipped tone. "Who on earth would ever look at you and think I'd only date you out of pity? *Honestly*." He's so irked, he's continually shaking his head and making disgusted sounds. "You don't think that, do you?" Suddenly, he's holding my hands earnestly, looking worried.

"Of course not," I reassure him. "In fact, I laughed at her. It's ridiculous."

He visibly relaxes. "Good. Because if anything, you took pity on me by agreeing to go on our first date."

"I disagree. But even if that were true, that would make you the best pity fuck I've ever had," I joke, trailing my fingers down his chest and looking up at him from under my eyelashes.

He raises an eyebrow, unimpressed. "Do you really need the qualifier?"

I laugh and smack him lightly on the

chest. "I'd say no, but apparently your ego is already big enough."

"You have no idea," he murmurs before planting a light kiss on my lips. "Have you eaten?"

I nod. "Just. I have more if you'd like me to make you a plate."

"You mean a plate of the food I cooked yesterday?" he teases.

I wrinkle my nose at him. "As a matter of fact, yes," I reply haughtily.

"Sure, that sounds good," he agrees. "I'm just going to …" He sinks back into the cushions and closes his eyes. Clearly, it's been a long day. I'm not usually the type of woman to wait on a man, but he did pretty much cater to my every need yesterday, so it's the least I can do.

So I not only heat him up some food, I also rub his feet while he eats, watching him hork the meal down with gusto.

"Boy, you really were hungry." I press my lips together to hide my smile, but he gives me a look, clearly getting that I'm making fun of him.

"I hardly ate, I was so slammed today.

Apparently, so much so that I missed all the gossip. But don't worry, I'll handle *that* particular issue tomorrow."

"Oh?" I ask, raising an eyebrow. "How exactly are you going to do that?"

Cal sets his plate aside with a wide grin. "Let's just say I've been trying not to seem overly interested in you so we didn't draw attention to ourselves. I think it's high time that stopped." I give him a skeptical look, still not sure exactly what he means to do, but all he does is laugh and pat the cushion next to him. "Shall we cuddle and watch a movie until I have to go home?"

I snort. "What are you, a fifteen-year-old girl?" I stare at him for a moment, trying to decide how to suggest an alternative. But he's a guy, so I just go for it. I stand up, remove my top, and settle on his lap. "I had a different sort of entertainment in mind."

"Fuck, Sasha," he groans, skimming his hands over my back. "I think I've died and gone to heaven." His mouth covers mine, and he wastes no time finishing undressing me. And while I don't get any more studying done for the rest of the night, I can't exactly say I mind.

Even though I pressed, Cal still wouldn't tell me what he was going to do. So when I arrive at work the next morning, it's with a nervous sort of energy, not knowing when or how his plan will be enacted. And while Becca doesn't say a word to me, she does acknowledge me with a nod. I'll take it, as at least it's not impolite or snarky.

Jules pops around the corner, and it's the first opportunity I've had to stop her since yesterday morning.

"Hey," I greet her.

"Hey, babes," she casually tosses at both Becca and I. Becca gives her a small wave without even looking up, and Jules raises an eyebrow as she hangs up her jacket.

I shake my head slightly, warning her not to ask right now. "So thanks for trying to give me the heads up, but I pretty much got the message through the rumor mill yesterday anyway," I tell her.

"Ah. Yeah, sorry about that. Yesterday was nuts," she apologizes.

I wave a hand dismissively. "For all of us, don't worry."

"What I'd like to know is, why you didn't tell me you two went out?" she says pointedly, crossing her arms over her chest and giving me a mock-stern look.

I chance a glance at Becca, who is pretending to focus on her computer screen. "We just needed some time to ourselves first," I explain. "You know, just to see if it went anywhere."

Jules makes a noise in the back of her throat. "Oh please, anyone who has seen you two together could've told you it was going somewhere fast. At least now the eye-fucking can stop. Publicly, anyway."

"You're not mad at me for keeping it from you?" I ask, trying not to sound as if I'm making a point to someone else who is still pretending not to pay attention. But I'm also extremely glad she clearly didn't believe the rumors for a minute. It gives me hope that maybe there are others who didn't either. Not that it really matters, I guess.

Jules, for her part, considers my question for a minute. "Well, you know me, I still want to hear the juicy details. But maybe one day after work. It'd probably be too weird to talk about it here. In any case, I'm not offended. You're a private person, Sasha, we all know that. I just want you to be happy."

Truly moved by her words, I step forward and hug her. She's surprised for a moment, but quickly hugs me back. "Thanks, Jules," I murmur.

"Of course," she replies. "Now let's get our gorgeous selves into the staff meeting and ignore the gossip-mongers who clearly don't know their ass from a hole in the ground." She starts dragging me down the hall, but a few paces in notices Becca not following. "Hey, grumpy pants. Your gorgeous self was included in that statement. Now stop acting like you weren't listening to every word, pull the stick out of your butt, and let's go."

I stifle a laugh, not wanting to piss off Becca more than she already is based on the look on her face. But she begrudgingly rises, stepping to Jules' other side and going with us to the meeting. Albeit silently, but I'll take it.

And I'm suddenly filled with hope. Hope that Jules can warm Becca up to forgiving me. Hope that whatever Cal plans to do will get people to leave us alone. And hope that Cal … well, that he's everything I think he is. That's the scariest of all, because I'm already falling for him. Hard.

When we get to the meeting, Cal's already there. That's surprising, given that he's almost always late. He's leaning against the far wall, talking to Dr. Carson. I swear the man should be a scrubs model. Cal, of course, not Dr. Carson. The way the material pulls across his pecs and skims his hard abs, giving just enough of a hint as to what's underneath is beyond distracting.

As if he senses me ogling him, he looks up and a huge grin breaks across his face. He excuses himself and comes toward me.

"Hey," he greets me, looking down at me with a smile. He's closer to me than he usually is at work but keeping enough distance to not cross any lines.

"Hey," I reply, dreamily staring up at him. It's hard not to when he turns that smile on me. It makes me understand the phrase "weak in the knees" just a little better every time.

He leans in, putting his mouth by my ear. His soapy-hospital smell envelops me, reminding me of waking up covered in his scent. "I missed sleeping next to you, beautiful."

He straightens up, his gaze locking on mine again, and I've never wanted to kiss him more. His face tells the same story, with his eyes darting to my lips, his teeth grabbing his bottom lip and pulling it into his mouth. A smile creeps across my face as I realize that this was his plan. Simple, effective. Because as Jules pointed out, anyone paying attention could see how much we want each other. Though she was wrong about the eye-fucking stopping at work. If anything, it might be worse now, because I know exactly what actually fucking him is like.

We're interrupted by a booming Dr. MacDougall calling our attention to the front. I don't miss that Cal and I are the first ones to do so. It takes everyone else a moment to tear their eyes from us and focus on our chief. I hear Cal chuckle lowly beside me, clearly pleased that his plan seems to have worked.

"Your little demonstration this morning backfired."

I look up to find Harper leaning over the counter of the nurses' station. I give her a steely glare.

"I'm sorry, are you referring to something having to do with our jobs? Because if not, I'm not interested," I reply icily. I'm still pissed at her for starting the rumors, even if I'm not entirely sure of how much of the story concocted was her or Lacey.

Harper slinks around the counter, crouching next to me and whispering. "Look, I'm sorry I told Lacey and Avery about seeing you two at the sushi place. But that's all I did, I swear. I'm sure you know Lacey hates you. And that she's been after Dr. Thompson since he started here. Which is why what you two did this morning was a bad idea." She looks around nervously, clearly terrified that someone is going to catch her ratting out her friend to the enemy.

Against my better judgment, I'm curious what she means. "Why was it a bad idea?"

Harper shakes her head. "I think she had really convinced herself he couldn't actually be interested in you, and still, look at the story she came up with to try to get you to stay away from him. Now that she knows he *is* interested ..." She looks around again and drops her voice even lower. "I've never seen her this angry or this fixated on someone. She won't shut up about you. She's been saying the nastiest things all day. I think she's going to try to get back at you, or break you guys up or something."

I shudder with disgust. "How can you even be friends with someone like that?" I hiss back.

Harper shakes her head. "I don't know. She's not always like this. But after this ..." She looks up at me desperately. "I'm really sorry. Just watch your back, okay?"

I shake my head, utterly sickened by the drama. "Fine. Thank you for the warning."

With a nod, she sneaks away, quickly disappearing down the hallway.

I sit at the desk, staring at the monitor blankly, completely unable to focus on what I was doing. I check Cal's schedule and see that he'll have a break after his current appointment, so I go and leave a note on his desk to page me at the nurses' station when he's free.

Thankfully, I don't have to wait long, and not ten minutes later I'm headed into his office.

"Hey," I greet him, closing the door quietly behind me. "I'm sorry, I know this isn't the best way to do this, but I have class tonight and I needed to talk to you."

He rises from his chair, skirting around his desk to meet me. "Are you okay?" he asks, his voice laced with concern and alarm.

"I'm fine," I assure him, laying a hand on his arm. "But you need to know what Harper told me." I relay everything to him, and the creases in his forehead deepen.

"Well, that's disturbing, but I'm afraid there's not much to be done for it," he murmurs.

"I agree, but I thought you should know,"

I reply. "And also … I had to ask: Harper said Lacey has been after you. Has she done anything that I should know about?"

His eyes meet mine, and they're suddenly flat and unamused. "Do you tell me every time a man flirts with you?"

I jut my chin out. "No, but this is different and you know it."

He shakes his head and sighs. "She has heavily hinted that she would like to see me outside of work. I'm always polite in return, never rising to her bait, and quickly getting things back in line if she wanders toward anything less than appropriate for coworkers. But yes, she's clearly interested."

"I saw you talking to her at the pub that time. If a man displayed that kind of focus toward me, I'd think he was interested in me," I point out.

He throws his hands up. "Americans. You're polite, you take care to pay attention to the words coming out of their mouths, and they think you just want to get them in bed," he says heatedly.

"Shhh, keep your voice down," I caution. "She's young, Cal. And extremely immature, if you hadn't noticed. If she likes you, she's going to take *any* attention you give her as encouragement."

"Isn't she about your age?" he asks shrewdly.

"Yes, I'm only a few years older than her," I allow, still seething. "But age doesn't dictate maturity. And that was *so* not my only point."

"Fine. You're right. Is that what you want to hear?" he snaps.

My eyebrows shoot up. "Well, I didn't think of this as an argument I was trying to win," I retort. "But yes, I'm glad to hear you agree with me." I stare at him for a moment, finally registering how agitated he is. "You really don't like explaining yourself or answering to someone, do you?"

He folds his arms over his massive chest defensively. Bingo. There's the surgeon's ego. Finally. I was starting to wonder.

I take a deep breath and step into him, running my hands over his arms, up to his shoulders before resting them on his traps.

"I trust you, Cal, that's not what this is about. But if you're not careful, she could ruin your career," I explain. "Just one accusation, one time where you're alone with nobody to prove what happened."

He lets out a breath and drops his arms, pulling me to him. "You're right. Of course, you're right," he agrees, kissing my forehead. "I'm sorry."

I can't help grinning into his chest. "Say it again," I tease.

He tilts my chin up to look me in the eyes and gives me a gentle kiss. "I'm sorry. You're right. You're a goddess, my Lada, my Venus, my Aphrodite. I bow before you, your humble servant, yours to command." A smile tugs at his lips and his eyes twinkle.

"That's more like it," I reply imperiously. "You may kiss me now, servant."

With a chuckle, he obliges, his lips meeting mine in a slow, sensual, yet mostly chaste kiss. When he's done, he leans his forehead against mine.

"To be continued," he promises. "Now get out of here before I'm forced to fully worship every inch of you."

"Promises, promises," I mutter as I pull away.

He laughs and shakes his head as he returns to his desk. I slip out of his office quietly, returning to the nurses' station. And though I felt the need to warn Cal, I can't help feeling like he's not the one who needs to worry the most.

13

The rest of the week creeps by, eerily uneventful. It's not until Friday morning, when I'm supposed to be off work, that I get a call from Dr. MacDougall asking me to come to the hospital and see him in his office. Grimly determined, I head in, prepared to face whatever bullshit Lacey has concocted to warrant this. Because really, what else could it be?

But when I enter his office, Lacey isn't there. Instead, an older woman with a severe gray bun and an equally severe black suit sits off to the side of the room.

"Dr. MacDougall," I greet him formally.

"Ms. Suvorin, please have a seat," he

replies just as formally. "I'm afraid we have something rather serious to discuss."

Even though I knew something like this would happen eventually, my heart still pounds in my chest as I perch on the edge of the black plastic chair in front of his desk. I glance to my left at the other woman.

"That's Mrs. Knowles, she's from administration and will be assisting with our, er, discussion today," Dr. MacDougall grumbles. He folds his hands together on the desk, looking sternly at me. "Now. You won't have known this, but pain medication has been going missing from the stores for some weeks now. We've implemented measures to determine the cause, to no avail."

"What about the cameras? And the logs?" I ask carefully. Though I know how easy it would be to "lose" pills or other forms of narcotics in a way that would escape notice. So many of us have access, and some level of pain management is necessary for most of our procedures.

"Yes, well," he hems and haws, "unfortunately, those weren't able to direct us to the culprit." He shifts uncomfortably. "But that's neither here nor there."

"I'm sorry, why am I here?" I ask bluntly.

"Because someone witnessed you stealing narcotics."

I almost laugh, but I stop myself just in time. Really? This is all she's got. Next, I *almost* accuse Lacey of "witnessing" this. But then, she's not completely stupid, so in all likelihood she convinced someone else to report it.

"I categorically deny that accusation," I reply firmly, meeting Dr. MacDougall's and Mrs. Knowles' eyes each in turn. "I have never stolen *anything* from this hospital, much less narcotics. That is a very serious claim."

"Indeed," Mrs. Knowles agrees. "Which is why I will be escorting you directly for an in-house drug test. If it is as you say, then you have nothing to worry about." She rises from her chair.

I happily stand. "Lead the way," I reply confidently.

She tilts her head and examines me for a moment, then with a small shrug exits the room. I follow her through the unit, into the main hospital, then through to the labs. She asks for a female technician who then escorts me into a large restroom, where she instructs me in how the test will be conducted. And that she will be staying to ensure there is no tampering with the sample.

With a resigned sigh, I comply, knowing it's the fastest, and only, way to clear myself.

Afterward, Mrs. Knowles brings me to administration and seats me in a waiting area where a guard stands, informing me that the results can take up to four hours. I want to ask why I can't go home and wait for the results. But now that they've told me they think I've been stealing drugs, I'd imagine they think I'm a risk for cleaning them out and making a run for it. The whole thing is beyond infuriating.

After a half hour of flipping through magazines, I pull my cellphone out, but the guard stops me.

"You can't use your phone," he instructs me harshly. I give him an incredulous look and barely bite back a snappy comment about needing to call my buyers so they know my stash has been cut off. But lord, if it isn't tempting. It's all ludicrous.

A little over three very long hours later, Mrs. Knowles returns, grim-faced. She gestures for me to follow her and takes me into her office. The guard follows, and my stomach drops.

She seats herself behind a giant gray metal desk and gestures for me to sit. She slides a piece of paper across the desk.

"Your sample was positive for hydrocodone," she says flatly. "I'm afraid we have no choice but to terminate your employment, effective immediately. Hospital administration will determine what kind of charges will be brought against you, so please keep in mind that your behavior going forward could vastly affect the outcome of such a case."

She shakes her head dimly, but I'm still in too much shock to fully register what's happening.

"I'm sorry, you said my test was *positive*? For hydrocodone?" I ask incredulously.

"That's what I said."

"That's not possible," I reply as panic starts to well in my chest. "I've never even taken hydrocodone. And it's not something we treat our patients with in our unit anyway. How could I possibly be positive for something I've never taken and don't come into contact with on a daily basis?"

"Whether you admit it or not, hydrocodone is available to the cardiac unit, and it has been going missing. I'm afraid even if you aren't willing to admit to stealing it, your positive result alone is basis for termination. Along with a witness to your theft, I'm afraid the evidence is rather conclusive. I'm sorry, Ms. Suvorin." She slides another form across the desk. "These are your termination papers. You will be paid for hours worked to date, though the hospital will be pressing charges and any litigation may require monetary damages when judgment is passed down. You will be required to stay at least one hundred yards from hospital property at all times. You are not permitted to contact any of the hospital's staff. If you are found in violation of these terms until any potential charges are settled, it could dramatically increase penalties. Do you understand what I've explained to you?"

"I … no … I *don't* understand," I whisper, tears starting to fall. My mind is spinning, but it latches on to one phrase. "Are you telling me I can't contact any of my coworkers? Both of my best friends work here. My … I'm dating someone who works here."

Mrs. Knowles shakes her head sadly. "I'm afraid if you attempt to contact them that will count against you."

"But …" My insides clench, and I feel like I'm going to vomit. "But what if they contact me? Do I have to ignore them until I can prove this is all a mistake?"

Her expression tightens, and I can tell she thinks I'm lying. That I'm just a user trying to elicit sympathy.

"We cannot legally require that nobody from this hospital contacts you. But I would strongly advise you to stay away from anyone associated with Rutherford Hospital until all legal matters have been settled."

I look up at her through hazy vision as tears continue to spill out unbidden. "How long could that take?"

She rises. "In all likelihood, it will probably be a few months. I suggest if you value your career, you use the time to prove that you can turn things around. They'll almost certainly offer you rehab within the next weeks in order to expunge this from your record. I seriously recommend you consider that option."

I shake my head, tears flying. "What good is rehab to someone who has never taken anything stronger than ibuprofen?" The words are useless, but I can't help it, and I didn't say them for her anyway. I'm just dumbfounded by this turn of events.

The guard towers over me expectantly. Not wanting to make things worse, I comply, rising unsteadily and letting him lead me out of the building. I don't even think about how humiliating it is for him to watch me until I've driven off the property. But as soon as I have, I pull over and let the tears out. I cry for what feels like hours, until I'm delirious and dehydrated. And then I do the only thing I can think to do. I call my mom and cry some more.

It was the smartest thing I could do. She doesn't doubt my veracity for a minute and points out that if Lacey really is behind this, she would've anticipated that they'd drug test me. And that she must have figured out a way to tamper with that. The possibility seems outlandish; tampering with lab tests results is a serious offense. Almost worse than stealing drugs. But there's enough truth to her words that I decide to immediately take her next piece of advice and go obtain my own drug test at an independent lab. Thankfully, I know all of them in the area, since we often refer patients to labs nearer to their homes or workplaces.

I make a pitstop at a gas station and buy a humongous bottle of water. The time for blubbering is over. It's time to start proving I was set up. If that's even possible. But I'm sure as hell going to do my best to try.

EVEN THOUGH I'M ABLE TO GET IN AT another rapid-test facility, given the hours wasted at the hospital, my results from the independent lab won't be available until Monday. So I head home.

I sit in my living room, completely unable

to focus on anything, my nerves compelling me to pace. I pick up my phone what feels like a thousand times, but I know I can't text Cal. And it's driving me insane. Especially thinking about Dr. MacDougall announcing to everyone that I was fired for stealing narcotics and that nobody is to contact me. Or at least, that's how it goes in my head. Though we've had people fired for exactly that once or twice before, and it's usually done much more discreetly. Still, when it happens, news travels fast, and even without an announcement Jules, Becca, and Cal probably already know by now.

My mother had invited me to come stay with her and Dad until this blows over, but if I can't contact any of my friends, I want to be here in case they try to contact me. And when a knock comes at the door shortly after six, I'm glad I did. I open the door to see Becca, her cheeks streaked with dried tears.

She launches herself at me in the fiercest hug she's ever given me.

"Oh, Sasha," she breathes. "Are you okay?"

I squeeze her back, battling with the tears

threatening at the back of my eyes. I blink them away and clear my throat. "I've had better days. Tell me what happened today."

I let go and step back so she can come in. Being very familiar with my place, she heads into the living room and plops dramatically on the couch.

"First," she hedges, wringing her hands, "I need to apologize. Being mad at you for holding back your news about you and Cal was just petty and … and in the grand scheme of things, so, so stupid. I'm so sorry, Sasha. Can you forgive me?"

I scoot closer to her on the couch, putting a hand on her knee. "I already have. Now please, I'm dying here, what happened after I was escorted out of the hospital?"

"None of the higher-ups said anything," she says, answering the unasked part of my question. "It was all whispers and rumors, as usual. But the gist was all the same: You were accused of stealing drugs. They tested you and it came back positive, so you were fired."

I shake my head, willing the whole thing to be a dream. But I'm awake. And this is happening.

"Did you know I can't contact anyone? And they told me it would be better if I didn't talk to any of you if you contact me. Fair warning," I tell her.

"Will you get in trouble if I'm here?" she asks with wide eyes.

"How can I get in more trouble than being fired for drugs I didn't steal or take yet somehow tested positive for?" I growl, rubbing at my eyes. "I'm sorry, I'm not mad at you. This is just crazy."

"So you really did test positive? How the hell did that happen?" she asks.

"You have no idea how much I appreciate the implication that you don't think I actually took drugs," I reply.

"Holy shit, Sasha, of course I know you didn't. Anyone who knows you wouldn't believe you did."

I blink hard, again fighting tears. "Do you think Cal does?"

Becca shakes her head. "I don't know, hon."

I look up at the ceiling and sniff deeply.

"I went to another lab to get an independent test, but the results won't be back until

Monday. This is going to be the weekend from hell," I grumble.

"Well, good on you. Do you have any idea why the test would've come back positive?"

A sarcastic laugh rips out of me. "Are you kidding? Don't you know who started those ridiculous rumors about Cal only dating me out of pity?"

Becca gives me a look. "What does that have to do with this?" she asks, clearly confused.

I lay a hand on her knee. "Oh, sweet, innocent, Becca," I joke drily. "Let me tell you a tale that a little birdie named Harper whispered in my ear." And I tell her about Lacey's jealousy, Harper's warning, Cal's response, and even go back to their interaction at the pub as evidence that Lacey is bitter, immature, *and* delusional. Clearly a more dangerous combination than even I realized.

"Wow," Becca whispers when I'm done. "But even if that's true, how would she mess with your test?"

"I don't know," I admit. "My plan went as far as proving that I'm not on drugs. I'll submit that to hospital administrators on

Monday along with a statement about my interactions with Lacey and Harper, and my suspicions, and we'll go from there, I guess."

Becca shakes her head. "Lacey's played this well. If you write all this down, you're gonna make yourself sound like a serious crackhead," she points out.

"God, I hadn't even thought about it that way," I admit. "But you're probably right. What else can I do, though?"

"You leave that to me," Becca says with a determined expression. "Besides, you've got finals on Tuesday. Focus on that, okay?"

I scrub my hands over my face. "I'm not going to be able to focus on anything until I know where Cal stands on all of this."

Becca rolls her eyes and pulls out her phone. "Fine. Give me his number," she demands. I look at her like she's sprouted another head. "What? You can't call him, but I can. Gimme." She gestures impatiently. And I'm just desperate enough to hear his voice that I cave.

As it rings, she looks at me and mouths, *Will he answer?* Just as I'm about to reply that as long as he's not in surgery he always does in case it's an emergency, he picks up.

"Dr. Thompson," he answers curtly. And I could cry for hearing his voice, both from relief and longing.

"Hi, Dr. Thompson, this is Becca Dillon. I'm sorry to do this to you, but I'm calling on behalf of Sasha. As you probably know, she's not permitted to contact you, but I think you two really need to talk." Becca's tone is firm and businesslike, and I want to kiss her.

Cal is silent on the other end for so long that a worried lump starts to form in my throat. I hear a door close, and I picture him in his office. It only makes me remember being in there with him, and the memories crush my already fractured heart at the thought that it may never happen again.

"I appreciate your concern for your friend, Ms. Dillon, but as a doctor at Rutherford Hospital, I'm afraid I'm not allowed to contact nurses who have been fired for provable drug use, especially while matters have not yet been settled, legally speaking."

I've never heard him speak that harshly, not even to patients. His tone, his words, it all smashes the bits of my heart into even tinier pieces.

"Huh," Becca grunts. "That's a cute party line. But we're not just talking about any nurse here. We're talking about Sasha. The woman you're dating. The one who is sitting here looking like you just murdered her puppy."

My eyes grow wide and I shake my head violently.

"She's there with you? I'm on speaker-phone?" he asks sharply.

"She sure is, and you sure are," Becca responds flatly.

"Ms. Dillon, I'm afraid I can't continue this discussion at the moment as I'm *at work*," he replies pointedly.

"I see," Becca replies slowly. "So does that mean you'll be prepared to finish this discussion when you're *not* at work?"

There's another long pause. "I'll see that that's the case when I'm done here. I trust you are where I think you are?" he replies.

"If you think I'm at Sasha's apartment, then yes," she agrees.

"One more thing, Ms. Dillon."

"Yes, Dr. Thompson?" she replies with an airy, mocking tone.

"It is best if we all *officially* keep our distance until matters are settled. Do I make myself clear?"

"Crystal. I'll take myself, my devastated and *wrongly accused* best friend, and our *unofficial* business out of your hair now."

She hangs up before he has a chance to say anything else, and I can tell it's because he royally pissed her off and she doesn't want to make things worse.

"It's a good thing he's so goddamn hot, because right now I don't know what else you see in him," she snips.

I shake my head slowly, not even really hearing her. My mind is working on parsing what he said.

"What if he's just protecting me?" I hazard.

Becca scoffs. "Girl, did you listen to a word he just said? That man is protecting *himself*. He's a damn doctor. I should've known he would. They don't know anything but their jobs. I'm surprised he'd even risk agreeing to come here. If I were you, I'd get the one-up and kick him to the curb before he can do it to you. I guess we found out why we have that rule, Sash. Never date a doctor. Apparently, they only look out for themselves."

"You're wrong about him," I protest. "You'll see." But given everything that's happened, I can't even say I'm right.

Becca leans in, catching my eye and putting a soothing hand on my shoulder. "I get it. You need to hope right now. And I don't want to see you get hurt, but that man has 'hurt' written all over his gorgeous self. Just be prepared, okay?"

"Okay," I agree.

"Good. I'm gonna scoot on out of here and start working on taking down that bitch, Lacey. And so I'm not around to kill your man when he gets here. I'd say call me if you need to, but …"

"Yeah. Thanks anyway. I'll probably be studying the rest of the weekend, like you said. There's not going to be anything else to do."

"Chin up, boo. We're going to clear your

name, I promise," she says, rising. I stand with her, and she wraps me in a hug.

As I see her out, I'm glad that this has at least brought us back together. Especially because it seems like things with Cal are going to be precarious, at best.

In anticipation of a painful conversation, I continue my pacing, too stressed to eat, watch TV, or focus on anything in particular. It feels like a lifetime before I hear the doorbell.

And when I open the door, he's leaned against the frame with one arm, looking haggard. He doesn't attempt to come in, kiss me, or even smile at me.

"Hi," I say softly, tentatively.

"I take it Ms. Dillon isn't actually here any longer?"

I shake my head. "No, she's not. Do you want to come in?"

He sighs heavily and nods, running a hand over his beard. "Probably best to do this in private."

The knots in my stomach tighten, and I have to breathe to keep from freaking out. I follow him into the living room, where he settles on the opposite end of the couch from me.

He gestures to the bandage on my inner elbow. "They did a blood test?" he asks, clearly curious.

"Not at Rutherford. After … after they let me go, I had my own independent testing done, on every bodily fluid they use. I'll get the rapid results on Monday," I explain.

"I presume you're attempting to prove you aren't, in fact, using drugs, then?" he asks.

My throat constricts and I shake my head sadly. "Did you really think I was?"

He scrubs his hands over his beard again, then through his hair. "I don't know what to think about anything anymore."

Ouch. I decide I'll come back to that one later. "Did you mean what you said? That you can't be in contact with me while this is unresolved?"

His hands settle over his mouth as he stares down, seemingly contemplating his answer. Finally, he drops his hands, blows out a breath, then lowers his chin. "Yes," he replies, refusing to look at me.

"They said it could take months," I reply. I

hear the weakness, the longing in my voice, and it just makes this so much harder.

"While there's a possibility that this could affect my career, I can't take that chance. I hope you understand."

"You mean while there's a possibility that I'm an addict, you can't take the chance on me."

He looks at me blankly. "Something like that, yes," he admits.

His words are like a punch to the gut. "God, Becca was right about you. They were all right about you. I should've never agreed to go out with you." The words tumble out, but it's too late to regret them. It's how I feel about what he said. About the selfishness of his words. "Never mind what *I'm* going through right now, I'm just a druggie. It's *your* career that's important. God, I'm so stupid."

"I don't blame you for being angry with me," he admits, finally looking up at me. "I'm angry with me. But it's a chance I can't take."

"Believing me? Trusting me? You can't take that chance? Well, I guess at least this shows me exactly where I stand with you."

"I wish I could just believe you, but I've never seen a drug test lie before. Though if somehow you are telling the truth, this could all blow over before —"

"*If* I'm telling the truth?" I snap. "Are you serious right now? God, I *am* stupid. And blind. Even if this blows over soon, there's no taking this back, Cal. And if it takes longer, well, you're still a selfish asshole who thinks I'm a liar and a user because some *test* told you that. Never mind what I say." I stand up, unable to take anymore. "Please leave."

He looks up at me pleadingly. "Please, Sasha," he says, his voice finally breaking. But it's not going to break me. I remain standing, refusing to back down. "I want to believe you. Really, I do. But … I just can't afford to. I wish you knew how sorry I am."

I glare at him furiously. "Seriously, feel free to take your pity party elsewhere," I seethe. "You clearly don't give a shit about what this is doing to me or the words coming out of my mouth. It's all about you. I see that now."

He rises, getting in my face. "I do care

about you. That's why this is so difficult. Don't you see that?"

"No, Cal. All I see is you, not believing me and doing what's best for your career." I march out of the living room and open the door. "Please, just go."

He moves slowly into the foyer, his face a mix of emotions. I clench my jaw and jut out my chin, stubbornly refusing to cry. With one last pleading look, he goes. And as soon as I close the door behind him, I slide down to the floor and let it all out.

"What do you mean, results won't be available until tomorrow?" I ask tightly into the phone. "I specifically requested rapid results on the urine sample." I listen impatiently to the woman on the phone apologize and insist that it wasn't checked on the submission, but that results for all the tests will be available by close of business tomorrow. In the grand scheme of things, another day isn't going to change much, but it's just another disappointment.

When the call is over, I chuck my phone onto the couch and rub my temples fiercely. And then I do what I've spent the last two days doing and bury myself in studying. Because if I can't control the shitstorm that is this drug test debacle, I'm sure as hell going to ace my finals.

———

I FINALLY GET THE CALL TUESDAY AFTERNOON that the results are in. I drop by to pick up physical copies, then ask them to send the results electronically to Mrs. Knowles' office. I take pictures of the paperwork with my phone and email them to her myself too, letting her know that she'll be receiving them directly from the lab as well, and that I would appreciate her reviewing the results and explaining why, just hours after Rutherford's tests, another, more complete round of lab tests shows not a trace of any kind of drug in my system.

I head to campus, finally feeling like I might be getting some traction. I'm a bit early, but I spend the remainder of the afternoon in the library, doing some last-minute review.

When I head to class, I'm confident that I'm about to nail my tests. Then just one more quarter and I'm a qualified nurse practitioner. At least that's something.

But as soon as Professor Chaffin sees me, he scurries over before I can take my usual seat.

"Ms. Suvorin," he says, a note of panic in his voice, "what are you doing here?"

My heart sinks. "What do you mean?"

"I take it you haven't checked your university email this week?"

"I guess not," I reply, realizing I haven't. "Why?"

I can see him starting to sweat behind his giant, thick glasses. "I'm sorry, Ms. Suvorin, but the hospital contacted us regarding your termination. Due to the nature of the circumstances, you've been removed from the program."

My jaw drops in shock. "You've got to be kidding me," I reply. "When?"

"Yesterday. I'm sorry, but as I'm sure you know, the reasons for your, er, termination were also a violation of the student code of conduct, so they were ethically bound to notify us."

I close my eyes and take a deep breath. "I

literally have test results right here," I rummage in my bag and produce the papers, "proving that their 'reasons' were incorrect."

His lips thin and he takes the papers from me. Clearly, they filled him in on *exactly* why I was fired, which frankly seems like a breach of privacy to me, as he quickly peruses them before declaring, "I see what you mean. Unfortunately, this is something you'll have to take up with the dean's office. It's out of my hands."

I want to stomp my foot, punch a wall, anything to blow off the steam building in me. I snatch the papers back from him and leave without another word. Nothing that comes out of my mouth right now is going to be good.

I go home. And wait. With literally nothing to do. No work, no school. For the rest of the week I alternate between crying and throwing things, hearing from nobody. Not even the hospital, despite repeated attempts at contacting them to follow up on the paperwork I submitted. So clearly they have no plans to un-fire me.

On Friday I finally decide to take my parents up on their offer and spend two days wallowing in my childhood bedroom, watching TV, and eating comfort food.

Come Monday morning, my mother drags me out of bed.

"Up," she insists, yanking the pink comforter I picked out in eighth grade off of me.

"Why?" I groan.

My mother crosses her arms over her slim chest. "You've done enough waiting. Now we do."

I open my eyes and sit up, curious. "Do what?"

"I'm taking you to a lawyer. If the hospital won't respond to you, you need to do something to clear your name. Even if you decide not to keep working there."

I frown at her, my mind working slowly on her words. She makes me realize that I've let the negative momentum of my pity party take over, and it pisses me off enough to get me out of bed.

"You're right. Thanks, Mom."

With a satisfied nod, she leaves me to get showered and ready.

When I come out for breakfast a bit later,

Dad's already gone to work. Mom waits patiently for me to eat, then we're off.

MONDAY AFTERNOON FINDS ME BACK AT MY apartment. And while the lawyer did advise that I continue to not contact my friends and Cal, they seemed confident that this was an open-and-shut case. They'll write an official letter to hospital administration today and follow up with a phone call tomorrow. At worst, they will have to meet with the hospital attorneys to see if there was anything holding them up from clearing me. At best, it will scare them into responding to my original request for an explanation regarding the discrepancy between the two tests. Which hopefully will lead to them admitting they wrongfully terminated me.

And while the continued wait is near maddening, at least this time it's with some hope.

I'm not disappointed when, midday Tuesday, the lawyer calls me. Turns out the hospital has been investigating my original test this whole time and has asked for another business day to wrap up their findings. Based on their language, I suspect they know why but can't tell me.

So I wait. Some more. I finally decide to wander to the diner down the street for lunch on Wednesday, just to get out of the house. The pleasant March afternoon does wonders for me, and on my way back to my apartment, my cellphone rings.

"Hello?"

"Ms. Suvorin, this is Edward Nolan, Mr. Gomez's legal aide."

"Yes, of course," I say, freezing in place with nerves.

"I'm calling to let you know that we've come to a resolution with Rutherford Hospital administration. They have rescinded your termination and you will be back in rotation starting this coming Monday, with full pay for the hours you were denied. We've also contacted the dean's office at your school to let them know, and hospital administration should be following up with them as we speak. They should be contacting you soon to schedule makeup exams ahead of the next quarter starting in just over a week."

"That's great, but did they say why my original drug test came up positive?"

"Unfortunately, they were not able to elaborate on what caused the issue." He clears his throat. "But we've been assured that the matter was fully investigated and appropriate measures have been taken to avoid such problems in the future. Now, as advised, we wouldn't recommend pursuing any additional damages in this case, but if your feelings on the matter have changed, please do let us know before you start back at work, otherwise doing so will signal acceptance of their terms."

"I understand," I reply. "Does that mean I can call my friends that are coworkers now?"

"It does."

"Thank you," I breathe in relief.

"It's been my pleasure to assist, Ms. Suvorin. Do you have any further questions at this time?"

"No. I appreciate your help very much."

"All right then, take care, and do let us know if you need anything else."

I end the call, still frozen. It takes a minute to sink in. I'm cleared. I can go back to work. I can go back to school. I can call my friends. Unfortunately, both Becca and Jules are working today, so I doubt I'll get ahold of them immediately. But my fingers are already flying, texting them both with the news.

Admins admitted the test was wrong. I'll be back Monday!

And then I practically skip home, on cloud nine. Until I realize that doesn't change anything between Cal and me, and I come crashing back to earth. So when school calls to reschedule my exams for next Tuesday evening, it at least gives me an excuse to go back to doing one of the things I do best — studying. Even though I pretty much know the material backward and forward at this point.

I hear from both Becca and Jules that evening, and we schedule a happy hour meetup for tomorrow. They pick a bar a couple blocks away from our usual, making me wonder.

I don't spend too much thought on it until Thursday evening as I get ready, slipping into something a little nicer than the sweats and tees I've been wallowing, er, living, in since the shit hit the fan.

And when I show up at the noisy dive they've chosen, I can tell by the looks on their faces that they've got something juicy to share. Becca is practically vibrating out of her chair. Until she spots me, that is, then she vaults to her feet and throws herself at me.

"Oh, I'm so glad to see you," she gushes. She squeezes hard and rocks me back and forth until I'm laughing.

"Oof," I tease. "I can tell."

She pushes away and sticks her tongue out at me. Jules approaches less violently and gives me a gentle hug.

"It's been awful at work without you," she whispers in my ear. She pulls back, gesturing to the third seat at their table. "We saved a chair for you. It wasn't easy." She sounds like she's teasing, but looking around at the bustling tables and the raucous crowd around the pool tables, I'm thinking she's also kind of serious.

"Why's it so busy in here on a Thursday?" I ask as I take a seat.

"Spring break," Becca explains, taking a sip of her drink.

"Ah. To that end, I get to take make my finals up next Tuesday."

"That's great," Jules says warmly, reaching out and squeezing my hand.

"So, spill. What's going on? Why'd we meet here instead of the usual?"

Jules shoots a look at Becca.

"We didn't want to take a chance that anyone we work with would be here. There have been rumors about what happened with your drug test," Becca explains. "When they reinstated you yesterday, someone in the lab was fired. You do the math."

"They tampered with my test?" I ask incredulously.

Jules shrugs. "Those are the rumors. But you know, grain of salt. Well, boulder of salt when it comes to Rutherford. Who knows what really happened? It could've been something as simple as mislabeling or entry error. But either way they clearly felt they had to fire the person responsible."

My stomach sinks a little thinking an unintentional error might have led to someone being fired because of me. But then ... "No. No, Jules. This had to have something to do with Lacey." The certainty forms in my gut.

Becca nods in agreement. "I think so too, even if Jules wants to give people the benefit of the doubt. But I have a small piece of good news on that front. Harper has agreed to try to get the truth out of Lacey. If she finds out Lacey had something to do with faking your drug test, she's going to turn her in."

I scoff. "Lacey's not completely stupid. She's not just going to admit to something like that."

Jules shrugs. "It's our best shot without doing something sketchy."

I shake my head. "Whatever. I'm back at work. They're not about to throw any more accusations at me lightly. And Lacey's plan worked. I'm not seeing Cal anymore. She can have him as far as I'm concerned."

"What?" Jules gasps. "Why?"

I smack myself in the forehead. "Crap, I forgot I haven't been able to talk to you guys," I say with a sigh. I tell them all about my last conversation with Cal. Becca is, predictably, furious.

"See," she insists. "Never date a doctor. That guy is bad news, Sasha. I'm so sorry."

Jules just looks bewildered. "He never seemed like such a jerk," she muses. "I mean, I can understand him wanting to protect his career, but not believing you? That's just bullshit."

"Exactly," I agree. "He obviously didn't know me at all. Or really care to. I guess I was just a piece of ass to him." I shake my head, my gut twisting at the thought. It didn't feel like that. It felt like we connected on just about every level. I've never been fooled quite this badly before, and it hurts.

"I don't know about that," Becca says, surprising me. But then she continues. "He's probably just not capable of thinking too much about anybody but himself." There she is. Though she kind of has a point.

"You're probably right. He's just a selfish *twat*," I reply, with a British accent on "twat." I flag down a waiter and order a drink. "Now, let's get our drink on and celebrate my coming back to work. And finding a way to stick it to Lacey. One way or another. Maybe her ending up with Cal would be a fitting punishment after all."

Jules gives me side-eye, clearly concerned at my vindictive switch. But I don't care. I may have been the type to rise above it all before, but this time the bitch has gone too far.

15

My studies over the next couple of days are interrupted by alternating thoughts of rubbing my innocence in Cal's face and getting back at Lacey. I know it's not productive, and I know I should just forget them both, but it stings. I mean, how could you not want to get back at people who have humiliated you? Lacey at work, and Cal … the words "in love" pop into my head, but I immediately choke on the thought. Love? No, I don't think I love Cal. Or … maybe I do, and that's why this hurts so much. The thought makes me sick to my stomach, so I stuff it down into the dark, deep places in my mind not to be examined too closely.

I'm thankfully distracted by Jules texting to ask if I want to meet for brunch tomorrow. I'm glad for an excuse to go back to the place Cal introduced me to, tainted with memories though it is. Because let's face it, the food was phenomenal. And I probably do need to get out of the house. Besides, Jules will be a much more calming influence than Becca would be. So I agree.

The next day, I know I've made the right choice as soon as the first bite of carnitas chilaquiles hits my tongue. I moan in pleasure and Jules laughs.

"That good, huh?" she teases, throwing her auburn hair over her shoulder.

I nod and gesture with my fork at her plate, since she got the same dish on my advice. She takes the hint and scoops up a bite of her own. And soon, she's moaning in delight too.

"Oh my god, you weren't kidding," she says, laughing around the mouthful of food.

"I don't kid about food," I say mock-seriously, then we both laugh.

"Well, if Cal introduced you to this place, at least one good thing came out of your relationship, right?" She continues to shovel down her food unapologetically.

I grimace and set my fork down. "Ugh. Can we not talk about it?"

Jules purses her lips. "Sorry." Her voice is muffled from her meal, and it makes me smile.

I shrug lightly. "Let's talk about me going back to work tomorrow. What's the temperature? Do people still think I'm a druggie? Or am I the poor nurse who was almost screwed over by the hospital?" My eyes go wide. "Does anyone even suspect Lacey has anything to do with it?"

With a laugh and a shake of the head, Jules sets her fork down and wipes her mouth with her cloth napkin. "Slow down, Sasha," she replies calmly. "No, they don't think you're a druggie. And I wouldn't say they think you were screwed over, but they are pretty suspicious about the whole thing. Nobody seems to have made any connection to Lacey, but then, why would they? I think they just think it was someone in the labs trying to cover their tracks for stealing the drugs."

I pick my fork back up and play with the food, eating a small bite and chewing thoughtfully. "I guess that makes sense. I pretty much figured Lacey wouldn't let it get back to her if she could help it. And there's almost zero chance she'll spill anything to Harper. Even if she did, I doubt there's any proof."

Jules eyes me suspiciously. "You're trying to figure out another way to take her down, aren't you?"

I drop my fork again and this time push my plate away. It says a lot about how agitated I am that I've just lost my appetite. "How could I not?" I seethe.

"Sasha," Jules says with a warning in her voice. "You don't know anything either." I go to protest, but she holds up a hand. "I agree, it's suspicious. But you have to work together. Start practicing your game face and *be patient*. If she really has done what you think she has, she'll slip up again, and she *will* eventually get herself in trouble. It's karma, babe. It'll come back to bite her in the ass."

I frown deeply, finding that line of thought

completely unsatisfying. "I'm just going to help karma do its job," I persist. "You know, so I can be there to witness it biting her in her annoyingly perfect ass."

Jules' eyes drift over my shoulder and her facial expression freezes.

"What?" I ask, moving to turn around.

"Don't," she hisses, grabbing my hand. "Speaking of Lacey's annoyingly perfect ass. I think she just sat down on the other side of the restaurant. And … oh, god …" Her mouth drops in horror.

"What?" I whisper insistently.

"I think she's with Cal."

Before I can stop myself, my head whips around. And she's right. Cal is sitting at a table across the restaurant, looking delicious in a white and gray rugby shirt and jeans, his hair freshly washed, smiling lightly at the woman sitting across from him. She has long, dark hair, just like Lacey, but something's not quite right … it's not Lacey, but she looks familiar. And she's got a ring on her left hand. On *that* finger.

"That's not Lacey," I say in a low, flat voice. "That's his fiancée."

"Don't you mean ex-fiancée?"

I close my eyes against the tears forming. "It would appear not."

The terror of the realization must show on my face, because Jules glances at a group of people next to us who are getting ready to leave, reaches into her purse, and throws a wad of bills on the table. As soon as they rise, Jules pulls me up with her, and drags me out the door, camouflaging us with their numbers.

Once we're outdoors, the panic really hits me, and I double over, clutching my knees and gasping for breath.

Jules rubs my back gently and eases me back a few feet to take a seat on a nearby bench. "Just breathe," she coaches.

I nod, focusing on calming myself down.

"Take your time," she says soothingly. "They hadn't even ordered yet, and they didn't see us. You're going to be okay."

It's all the things we're coached to say to people who are having a panic attack. And because I know that, this time it sets me off just a little more, and I can't fight the tears back anymore.

"It's not okay," I gasp. "I really was just a

blip on his radar. A distraction until he decided whether he really wanted to get back with her. Oh god, Jules, I'm such an idiot."

"You're not an idiot," she insists. I shoot her a sharp look. "Well, then we're all idiots. You're not the first girl this has happened to, Sasha. But I know that doesn't make it suck any less."

"No," I agree. "No, it doesn't. Can you just … take me home, please?"

Jules gives me one last pitying look and then nods. "Okay. Let's get you home."

BECCA IS ALREADY GOING FULL TILT WHEN I start back to work on Monday.

"I have a plan," she greets me gleefully.

I stare at her with dead eyes. "If it has anything to do with Lacey, just forget it. I'm done with all the drama. I just want to go back to my life."

"What happened?" she asks, pouting and clearly disappointed.

I shake my head, not ready to talk to her

about seeing Cal and his fiancée back together. Or spending all night sick to my stomach from crying and agonizing over seeing them. Saying I'm done with drama is an understatement. I just want to sink back into the familiarity of work and school and forget that anything else exists. Possibly even Becca if she won't let me be.

"Come on, Sash, I'm here for you, you know that," she says softly, trying to look a little less manic.

"I can't. Go ask Jules if you really want to know," I reply flatly. And with that I take my travel mug to get a refill. But I purposely go off-unit to a different machine, hoping to slip into the morning meeting via the back door once it's already started to avoid dealing with anyone or being noticed.

It was a great plan until I hear my name being called down the hall as I head for the meeting room. I look back to see Cal gaining swiftly on me.

"Sasha, wait," he calls, seeing that I'm not slowing down.

I dart for the door, but he's too quick for me, grabbing me by the wrist while I'm still a good ten steps away, spinning me around to face him.

"Let go of me," I growl in a low voice.

Alarmed at my response, he does just that, stepping back in surprise.

"You're back," he says obviously.

"Astute observation, *doctor*," I reply mockingly. "Now, if you don't mind, I need to get to the morning meeting."

"I do mind. We need to talk."

"We have nothing to talk about."

"I disagree."

"Hm. I think your *fiancée* might agree with me," I reply pointedly, glaring at him.

"Excuse me?"

I narrow my eyes and shake my head in disbelief. "You heard me. Your fiancée. Rachel? You know, the woman wearing your ring that you were having brunch with yesterday."

His lips press into a thin line. "You saw us?"

My stomach turns and I make a low sound of disgust in the back of my throat. "Yes, I did. Now, if you don't mind, Dr. Thompson,

I'd rather not give the vultures something new to taunt me with."

At the use of his formal title, he looks like I slapped him in the face. With grim satisfaction, I use his shock to my advantage and close the distance between me and the door, slipping inside without looking back. Thankfully, only a couple of people near the door notice, and I blend in. Cal never comes to the meeting. As disappointed as I am with the whole thing, I realize it's probably for the best.

THE WEEK IS AWKWARD AND UNCOMFORTABLE, to say the least, but thankfully I sail through my make-up finals and start the next quarter without a hitch. Cal avoids me, and Becca and Jules keep things light and perfunctory, letting me find my rhythm without anything extra. Back on plan, I bury myself in work and school, numbly surrendering to the demands of a packed schedule.

I ask Becca out for drinks on Saturday, but she declines, mysteriously citing "other plans." She's lucky I'm not her, or I'd be digging for details at the least, and stalking her for answers at the worst. But frankly, I'm fine having a few drinks by myself at home.

The rest of the weekend is blissfully boring, but by the time it's over and I decide I've had too much time to think, I'm ready to go back to work on Monday. Ready to take my mind off of all of this.

What I wasn't ready for was walking into chaos. Seemingly every nurse, medical assistant, orderly, and other employee on the unit is crowded into the hallway leading to the nurses' station. I press through the throng, wondering what the hell is happening. I look around for Jules, only to remember that she's off today. Instead, I find Becca, Harper, and Avery whispering angrily to each other behind the nurses' station counter.

I put a hand on Becca's shoulder. "What's going on?" I ask quietly. "What the hell is everyone doing out here?"

Becca turns to look at me, and it's then that I see the panic in her eyes.

"They just took Dr. Thompson away. I'm

so sorry, Sasha, I didn't mean for this to happen," she replies, tears welling in her eyes.

"What?" I screech. "Back up. You didn't mean for *what* to happen? Who took him where?" I glance between her and Harper, and they both look guilty as hell.

Becca glances at the crowd behind us that's already starting to dissipate. So whatever happened to Cal must have happened right before I showed up.

"Hospital administration and security showed up about ten minutes ago and escorted Dr. Thompson out of his office," she says in a low voice. "The why ... let's wait until everyone goes back to their stations, okay?"

I shake my head violently. "Tell me now, Becca. By the time they're gone we'll have to go to the morning meeting, then we'll be too busy to talk about it."

She hesitates just long enough that Sarah Marcus, our usual second shift nurse practitioner, comes tearing around the corner, looking less than pleased to be here so early as she shrugs out of her jacket and tosses her purse behind the counter.

"Morning meeting has been cancelled. Dr. Franklin has been called in to cover for Dr. Thompson. Get me the schedule for the day immediately," she commands.

Becca quickly grabs the clipboard she'd already prepared and hands it over without a word.

Sarah takes it with a grim nod. "I'll be in the break room guzzling the whole damn pot of coffee. I'll be back to go over this."

As she stalks away, the last of the stragglers take it as their cue that the spectacle is over and wander back to what they should be doing.

I whirl back on Becca, noting that both Harper and Avery have also slipped away.

"Spill it. Now."

"Fine," she agrees, pulling me to the back corner of the station. "Harper and I had a plan to get Lacey to confess on Saturday when we all went out for drinks after work. But it kind of backfired."

I hold up a hand. "*That* was your 'other plans'?" I demand.

"Yes," she admits with a sigh. "And if you had come it would've —"

"Stopped you from doing something incredibly stupid?" I interject. "What does that have to do with Cal?"

"He overheard us and he wanted to help," she responds, shifting uncomfortably.

"He *what*?" I say through gritted teeth. "Why on earth would he do that?"

Her expression shifts from guilt to tolerant pity. "Oh, Sasha, isn't it obvious?" she whispers.

I arch an eyebrow, determined not to rise to that bait. "Whatever. What did he do?"

She shrugs. "He just hung out with us. We all had a few. She was definitely laying it on thick, trying to get his attention. So he gave it to her. Everyone else eventually went home, and we left them there together."

My jaw drops in shock. Alcohol. Flirting. And Cal, who obviously sees women as his playthings. My stomach starts to churn thinking about what probably happened next.

"Don't worry, he didn't do anything with her," she assures me.

"How on earth could you possibly know that?" I snip, rubbing my temples. I internally scold myself for even caring. It doesn't matter. It's over between us, right? Then why does the thought upset me so much?

She puts her hands on her hips and looks at me smugly. "Because he texted me after he took her home. She admitted to him that she was the one stealing drugs. Well, her and her partner in crime in the lab, and that they were the ones who set you up to take the fall."

"How on earth did he get her to tell him all that?" I muse out loud.

Becca's eyebrows fly up. "You've seen him, right?"

I roll my eyes. "Whatever, I guess I don't really want to know anyway. So how did it go wrong? Why did they take Cal?"

She spreads her hands and shakes her head. "I don't know. But obviously Lacey's fighting back. I shouldn't have involved him."

I lean into the wall next to us. "He's a big boy. He can take care of himself. Better him in trouble than you."

Becca frowns. "Is that really how you feel? I'm just a medical assistant, Sash. I'm not that important, and I don't make a ton of money. I'm sure I could find some other job if

Lacey came up with some bullshit to get me fired. But she could ruin him."

I huff a short, unamused laugh. "I warned him that she could. You didn't force him to do anything, Becks. This is on him." I look up and catch her eye. "And you are important, you know. You do a lot around here. You know we all appreciate you."

"Thanks. But honestly, I'm starting to see things from his point of view, and how precarious his career really is. He put a lot on the line by going after Lacey's confession, Sasha. Maybe think about what that means."

"Maybe I don't care what it means. He didn't believe I wasn't a fucking drug addict," I seethe. "There's no point in thinking about things because there's no going back from that."

Becca's chocolate-brown eyes look pleadingly into mine. "He's only human. And I can tell he loves you. Why else would he do this? Risk himself like this?" I go to protest, but she literally puts her hand on my mouth. "And don't even tell me you don't care. You do, Sasha. You're not a cold-hearted bitch. I know you want to be because he hurt you, but deep down you're just not."

Footsteps warn us of someone approaching, so Becca slides into her seat behind the counter without letting me respond. Not that I'm sure I could if I wanted to. Her words have more truth in them than I'm comfortable with. Because deep down, I know I'm reacting this way out of hurt. And though I'm not sure forgiveness is in the cards, I do care about Cal. I say a silent prayer that he makes it out of this unscathed. So I can go back to ignoring him in peace.

THAT AFTERNOON, THE RUMOR MILL HANDS down that Lacey's been fired and walked out by security. Becca breathes a sigh of relief, presuming that means Cal is in the clear. But we don't see or hear from him the rest of the workday, so it's hard to say. His absence is unsettling. I chalk it up to not knowing exactly what's going on and get back to work.

Focusing is nearly impossible, though, and I end up having to reenter the same patient chart so many times I practically could've memorized it by the time I get it right. Clearly, my head isn't in it.

Getting off work isn't much relief either, and I'm distracted the whole drive home. When I make it to my assigned parking spot, I thank the universe for getting me home in one piece, as I remember little of the actual drive. I sit there for a moment, staring at the steering wheel, realizing I've been lying to myself about how much this has all upset me. But it's hard to put my finger on exactly why.

Shaking myself, I drag my ass out of the car and upstairs to my apartment.

I round the hall corner to my apartment and almost drop my keys in shock.

Cal, who is sitting on the floor with his back against my door, rises and dusts off his jeans.

"We need to talk."

I freeze in place. "I'm not ready to." The words sound choked and forced.

He crosses the distance between us, looking down seriously into my eyes. My insides twist and turn, part eating me alive with misery, part wanting to throw myself into his arms. My throat constricts when I recognize the desire, disgusted with myself for being so weak.

"Ready or not, it's time I told you the truth."

16

"Fine. Probably best to do this in private," I retort spitefully.

He shakes his head and huffs a breath out but says nothing. I push past him and unlock my door, holding it open behind me so he can enter. He closes the door behind him and follows me into the living room. I sink onto one end of the couch, crossing my arms over my chest defensively. I can feel the resistance inside me, even though part of me wants to hear what he has to say. I can only assume it's my instinct to protect myself, but I'm already confused and he hasn't even started.

He settles onto the other end, giving me as much space as he can.

"I need to start with the day you were fired," he says, scrubbing both hands over his beard. I gesture for him to continue. "Rachel contacted me that day. She wanted to meet as soon as possible to finalize things. She wants to get married."

My whole body cringes. "You mean you got back together with her before you even came over here and ended things with me? That's … I can't even …"

Cal looks up at me, confused for a moment before realization dawns on his face. "God, no, Sasha," he says in disgust. "She's marrying *someone else*."

He stares at me while that sinks in. He's not back together with her. He's not marrying her. She's engaged to another man.

"Oh my god," I gasp.

"Yeah," he agrees drily, wringing his fingers together. "Turns out she'd been cheating on me for a long time, but her parents were pressuring her to seal the deal with me. It explains a lot of her behavior, actually, but I have to admit it, uh, it didn't put me in a very trusting frame of mind for our conversation." He looks down into his hands, blinking hard like he's trying not to cry.

And it hits me. That's why he didn't believe me. A woman he'd loved for years had just told him their relationship was basically a lie. How could I, a woman he'd known only weeks, possibly expect his full and complete trust? Even without the bombshell she dropped on him, framing it in context of the shortness of our relationship makes me understand the events of that day just a little better, and I realize I probably overreacted. And I feel my confusion start to fade.

"I'm so sorry she hurt you."

He looks up at me, his blue eyes rimmed with red. "She didn't hurt me, Sasha. Not really. It was a shock, sure. But I'm upset because I let it get under my skin, and then I pushed you away because of it. You have no idea how sorry I am."

"So you two had brunch —"

"To finalize things. It's all done, and I never have to see her again. Thank bloody fucking Christ," he grumbles. "But as soon as I left you here that day, I wanted to kick myself. I know you wouldn't do drugs, Sasha.

God, I'm such a fucking idiot." He shakes his head, looking back into his hands.

"Thank you," I breathe. "For saying you know I wouldn't do drugs. Not for saying you're an idiot. Though, you know, you kind of were." He smirks in response, and I give him a tentative smile in return. "So what happened with Lacey? Becca told me you got a confession out of her."

"Ah, yes, that. She was drunk and trying to impress me, and it was surprisingly easy to coax her into telling me everything. I documented it all and took it to hospital administration. Naturally, they called Ms. Petersen in and levied the accusations against her. It was rather late in the day, though, so they weren't going to have conclusive drug test results on which to base a decision until today. She chose to attempt to further stall her termination by muddying the waters." I look at him, confused, so he adds, "She accused me of coming onto her in my office and saying if she didn't sleep with me, I'd make sure she was fired."

"*No,*" I gasp. "God, she's exactly as much of a scheming bitch as I thought she was."

"See, that's the thing," Cal replies. "You'd warned me about exactly that. So I had cameras installed in my office, as it's really the only place I'm ever alone. It didn't take long for her story to come apart after she learned that, even though it did rather add to the spectacle of it all."

"You listened to me," I say, touched that he actually took my advice.

"Of course I did. And I'm glad I could finally put a stop to her schemes. Now everyone will know what really happened and who's to blame. And hopefully anyone who still had doubts about you will feel as bad about it as I did."

"Is that why you felt like you had to help Becca and Harper get a confession out of Lacey? Because you felt bad for not believing me?"

He gives me a wry smile. "No. I did that because I love you."

My breath catches in my throat and my eyes go wide. "You … love me?"

Cal lets out a short, breathy laugh and his eyes glisten. "I do, actually. Damn, it feels good to finally tell you that." He slides toward me on the couch, and my stomach tightens with nerves. "From the moment I met you, I felt like I already knew you. Like we were meant to be. But I didn't want to say that and scare you off. And you reminded me of someone too, you know."

I stare at him as he settles next to me, completely unable to tear my gaze away. "You never mentioned that."

"I know," he admits. "Because it's stupid, really. My brother was going to school here, and I was visiting him on holiday. We went to the big airshow they have here every year and I saw this girl. Just glimpsed her through the crowd. She was the most beautiful creature I'd ever seen. She looked just like you — she had your same hair color, same height, same everything," he reaches out and tugs a dark blonde lock. "Then she was just gone. But I swear, that moment has stayed with me for years. And you didn't just remind me of her, but also of the feeling I had that day. And though that was ages ago, you could say I was already set to fall for you."

"Ten," I whisper as the tears start to fall. An ugly sob rips out of me, knowing I was right all along. Cal *is* Universe Guy. And I'd written him off so thoroughly and stubbornly that I didn't recognize my confusion and discomfort for what it was: the sadness of losing him. Because he's clearly meant for me. And I realize I already knew that on some level. And that I love him too.

"Ten what?" he asks, reaching up to wipe my tears.

"Ten years. It was ten years ago. Just outside the hangar. You were walking away from it with three other guys and wearing a blue shirt. I remember because it matched your eyes. Though you didn't have a beard then."

Cal's hand drops and he pales.

"You're not … there's no way …" he stutters, looking at me in disbelief. "That couldn't have possibly been you, Sasha. The odds —"

"Fuck the odds, Cal. That was me. And that's why I recognized you on your first day too."

"I was the one you had strong feelings for as a teenager?" he asks, astounded. "I thought you must've been referring to a first boyfriend or something."

"I *was* talking about you. I just didn't know it yet."

He shakes his head, still staring at me in disbelief. His hand finds mine, and he brings my fingers to his lips. "Please forgive me for being such an insufferable ass. I'm so sorry, Sasha. Even before I came here today I knew you were it for me. But now … fuck. This is just … it's incredible."

I close my eyes and take a deep breath. Breathing in the pain, the heartbreak, my stubborn, willful insistence on closing him out because he hurt me. Then I breathe out with forgiveness, love, and acceptance that you can only be hurt so deeply by those you love. And that the real lesson here isn't to never date a doctor; it's to let love in, no matter how much it scares you that you could be hurt. Because it's worth it.

"I forgive you." I open my eyes, free of tears for once, and entwine my fingers through his. "And I love you too."

His eyes shine back at me with everything I feel in this moment. He leans toward me, gently pressing his forehead to mine. I breathe deeply of his scent, allowing myself to sink into the moment as I wrap my hands around his neck.

Cal's hand gently strokes my cheek. "Say it again," he teases.

A grin breaks across my face. "I love you too."

His hands close on my face, tilting my mouth up as his lips claim mine. And I'm home.

Thank you so much for reading! Please take a minute to leave a review on any retailer, goodreads, and/or BookBub. Even if it's just a couple of sentences, your opinion is important to potential readers and to me. Thank you!

Want to see more of Sasha and Cal and find out what happens between Becca and the hot orderly? Get *Bad Boys Don't Make Good Boyfriends* (Book 2) now at https://melanieasmithauthor.com/books-bad-boys-dont-make-good-boyfriends.html

Sign up for Melanie A. Smith's newsletter to get a FREE book plus all the latest news and more https://melanieasmithauthor.com/ newsletter.html

ACKNOWLEDGMENTS

This was a slightly different undertaking than my usual project, and I found it more of a challenge than I'd anticipated. So above and beyond my usual process, I needed more reassurance overall. Goodness knows my husband is always first in the firing line when I'm in a panic and need to run an idea by someone. And even though he's already helping by even giving me time and space to write (no mean feat with a five-year-old in the house), he's always gracious and (mostly) helpful whenever I need to bounce ideas around or just have someone listen to me talk it out. So first thanks always go to him. I'm not the easiest person to live with at the best of times, much less when I'm in a creative crisis.

A huge thank you to my beta readers, Lindsey and Jacquie, for their eagle eyes on typos, spotting the exact issue I couldn't quite describe, and generally just being the best cheerleaders ever.

Always thank you to my editor and perma-BFF, Jenny. It's both amazing to get to do this with you and a little weird to have you edit my thank you (ha ha). In any case, I can't let it go without saying that your support even outside of editing has been crucial to this whole process for me, and frankly to my general development as a human being. Love you so much, babe!

I'd also like to thank Amanda McKinney, an amazing and talented indie author of some seriously steamy romantic suspense, who generously gave me access to her immense wealth of knowledge and experience. Her input has been crucial in reshaping my journey as an author, and I'm going forward with a confidence I hadn't had before.

And where would I be without readers? A huge thank you to each and every person who takes the time to read my books — even to those who don't love them, as there's something to learn from every reader who takes the time to provide feedback. But to those of you who *do* love them, don't be afraid to let me know. It's your enjoyment that keeps me going.

ABOUT THE AUTHOR

Melanie A. Smith is a former engineer turned stay-at-home mom and award-winning, international best-selling author of steamy contemporary romance. She crafts strong book boyfriends with hearts of gold and smart, self-sufficient heroines. When she's not lost in the world of books, you'll find her spending time with family, cooking, and driving with the windows down and the stereo cranked up loud.

facebook.com/MelanieASmithAuthor
twitter.com/MelASmithAuthor
instagram.com/melanieasmithauthor

Last Kiss Under the Mistletoe

Tough Love

Finding His Redemption

Vegas Baby (Hot Vegas Nights)

Pompous Paramedic (A Hero Club Novel)

Short Stories

Cruising for Love

Hot for Santa